I0570387

The Dragonrider's Quest

By

Daphne Ignatius

The Dragonrider's Quest

Copyright © 2014 Daphne Ignatius

All Rights Reserved

ISBN-13: 978-0692210581
Concertia Press
P.O. Box 697
Roswell GA, 30076

Table of Contents

Author's Note

Character thoughts and telepathic communication are denoted in italics without quotes.

(E.g. *How could this have happened, Lya?*)

1

Prologue

Ryce held up his robes as he picked his way down the narrow tunnel, winding into the depths of Bodian Mountain. He was irritated. His mother and her two apprentices had disappeared two days ago. Although that was normal behavior for his mother, the apprentices should have had the courtesy to keep him informed. He had spent over an hour in the library waiting for them to appear for their session. He had checked the castle and its grounds and, as far as he could tell, he was the only human above ground. That left only one place left to look. It was very odd for his mother to invite company into her workshop but then again, they rarely ever had company.

One foot slipped on the slick stairs and Ryce swore softly to himself. His shorter leg made it a challenge to go downhill in general, so he took the steps one at a time, leading with his good leg. With his luck, the seeping wetness would cause him to trip and break his neck.

The air became stale and damp as he proceeded downwards. The tunnel began to flatten out and he sighted the stout wooden door to the workshop. As he neared the door, the sour stink of mage-fire reached him. He smiled. Margary must have had little faith in her apprentices to have brought them this far underground to practice. The door didn't give, as it was locked from the other side. Ryce pounded on the door.

"Mother. Open the door!" he called through the solid wood. There was no response. He waited a few moments, then shrugged and turned to leave. As he did, it suddenly struck him that under the burnt smell; there was an undertone of sickly sweet corruption. He swung back around, and started pounding on the door. Not a sound from the other side. Making a quick decision, he backed away from the door and sent a blast of mage-fire streaming over the lock. Once it glowed red, he kicked it hard with his boot heel. The lock failed and the door slammed open to bounce off the rock wall.

The stench of decay flooded out. Heart slamming in his chest, Ryce stepped in to find his mother's workshop in shambles. Three bodies were on the floor.

"Gods!" Ryce gasped in horror, as he dropped to his knees beside his mother's body. She was lying on her side, hair covering her face, with a dagger sticking out of her back. Grief and fury rose to choke him. *What had the lads done to her? This was a complete betrayal of the master-apprentice bond!* One of them lay on his side, blue eyes open and glassy, flies crawling out of his mouth. The other was burned beyond recognition, dark red blistered flesh showing through the tatters barely covering his body. Ryce placed a hand on the body and sat back on his heels, when the body jerked slightly and responded with a moan of pain.

Alive? Ryce turned the survivor over onto his back, prompting another pitiful groan. Quickly, he placed a stasis spell on the burned apprentice, numbing his pain. He leaned over to cautiously open one eye to check for a response and rocked back again in dumb shock. The formerly brown eye had bleached to a silvery gray. Ageless. The survivor had somehow become ageless. *Obviously he*

3

must have forced my mother into sharing the secret of eternal life, but why had she complied? She could have destroyed him in a heartbeat. Nobody forces Margary of Bodian to do anything.

Ryce got to his feet, scanning the room for a weapon. He found a serrated knife in a pile of instruments on the table and moved back to stand over the wounded apprentice, breathing hard. His hand tightened on the knife. Vengeance. But something continued to bother him. Ryce got back on his knees and took a closer look at the wrists of the burnt man. When he realized what he was seeing, he grew cold inside. He could always kill the man later. First, he needed to learn what had happened here.

Ryce sat the unconscious man upright and then maneuvered himself until the man was propped on his back. He pulled the man's arms up over his shoulders, to hold him in place as he forced himself upright. Gritting his teeth in determination, he started hauling his load back up the stairs.

Chapter 1

The College of the Healing Arts, Huria

350 years later

The red dragon circled lightly above the stone-built cloister, standing proud on a small, green hill. Flax glanced up from sorting his herbs in the courtyard, as the dragon's shadow flitted across him. Backing away slowly under the gallery, he watched in awe as the majestic beast swept in for a landing in the middle of the courtyard. The dragon ignored him as it folded up its leathery wings neatly.

A woman swung off the dragon-saddle, dropped lightly to the ground and began to walk towards him. Her strawberry blonde hair was tied into an intricate braid, with a few tendrils blown loose to wave around her face. She was striking rather than beautiful, and very tanned from days flying in the sun. Eyes of grass and a body showing trim and subtly muscled beneath her ornate but lightweight armor. She was still young, but her overall look was intimating. Behind her, the dragon launched off the ground with a rush of wind.

The dragonrider came to halt, regarding the young apprentice gaping at her. "My name is Aenor Merivel. I bear a message from the Queen of Norwall for the Maester. It is of the utmost urgency." This in a voice, low and husky.

Flax suddenly came to life. "The Maester is outside the healing hall, my lady. I'll take you to him."

"Not quite a lady, I'm afraid," Aenor quipped with an encouraging smile. "Just a dragonrider."

"Apologies, my lady... dragonrider, I mean." Flax went to full blush as he gestured for her to follow him.

Marius, the Maester of the college, lay motionless on the grassy hillside a short distance from the sun-warmed cloister. His eyes were closed, his fingers dug into the soil at his sides as he drew energy from the sun and the ground beneath him. Above the stone cloister, rose the mountains that separated Huria from its northern neighbor, Norwall. There was not much here in this quiet corner of Huria that hinted at the political turmoil currently raging over the mountains. Apart from birdsong and the sound of the breeze, all was peaceful and the silence was a balm to his mind.

Each day, the healing hall would fill to capacity and he and his team of healers would clear it. The sheer predictability of it warred with the quiet sense of satisfaction that he still gained at the end of a hard day. So far, the satisfaction had won out each time.

"Maester," a teenager's voice broke into his reverie. Marius opened his eyes to find a pair of very green, very direct eyes looking into his. "A dragonrider is here from over the mountains."

Aenor managed to keep her jaws from falling into a childish gape. She hadn't put much thought into what the famed Maester of legend would look like, but the man lying at the feet certainly wasn't anything like she had expected.

This is a fit man in the prime of life! Long and lean, with nothing of the softness of a healer. His navy wool robes had ridden up his thighs to reveal black wool breaches tucked into soft leather boots that lovingly hugged the line of his muscled legs. The man looked more like a warrior poet than a healer who had lived for more than four hundred years.

The Maester swung easily to his feet with a polite smile, the hem of his robes dropping to fall to his knees. Thick black hair waved gently to his shoulders and his eyes were a silver gray. A short dagger hung from the wide leather belt at his waist.

"Norwall warriors don't cross into Huria without good reason," stated the Maester. "What has happened?"

Aenor blinked and pulled herself together. "My lord, I bring greetings from the Queen of Norwall and a plea for your help. Our prince has been wounded in an assassination attempt and lies at the brink of death. The queen asks for your help!"

The Maester cocked his head. "Warrior, you do know that I'm not welcome in your land, do you not?" he answered.

Aenor nodded her head. "That's why my dragon and I are here. We have been charged to get you to Miramar and back here in perfect safety. We will protect you with our lives, if we have to."

A brief flash of irritation crossed Maester's face. "Warrior, I know the Corp's reputation but you are no match for the Abida. We are not talking about men or beasts here, but elemental magic. Only a mage would be able to defeat them and I am not at full strength. He inconveniently senses my movements just as much as I sense his." The Maester fixed her with a stern gaze. "Are there none in Norwall that can serve the queen in the matter?"

Aenor stiffened her back, resenting the implied insult.

"Our healer, Astrid, is a former student of yours and she says that the prince is beyond her reach. The prince's body is intact but his spirit has departed to the Darklands. Astrid says that she's seen you walk the Darklands many times and bring back the dying."

The Maester nodded. "But I'm not the only one who can do so," he replied firmly. "You should look within your own country for aid. This is not my fight."

"Is there nothing that I can say or offer to change your mind?"

"This is not a decision that I make lightly. I'm sorry."

"So am I," Aenor murmured softly. She moved in a blur of color. The next instant, she was behind the Maester, holding her short sword to his throat. Flax yelled for help. The Maester merely stiffened.

"Warrior, *think* for a minute! Huria will not stand for this. Does Norwall really need more problems right now?"

"My orders are to get you to Miramar and I will. We'll deal with the rest later," she growled. "Now *move*!"

Aenor moved him swiftly towards the side door of the cloister that she had noted on the way in. All the while, her mind was racing. There was no way the mages in the cloister could stop her. They were healers. Weapons were forbidden to them, as were spells of attack. She wondered briefly why her captive had not blasted her with a spell of defense, but she chose to move on from that particular line of thought.

They moved out into the small, sunlit courtyard. There were already several blue robes milling around them but a single motion of the Maester's hand kept them from breaking their vows and picking up their gardening implements to defend him. Suddenly, a wall of rushing wind hit the healers, scattering them to the safety of the halls. Aenor screamed an order as she and the Maester stood firm against the buffeting winds. Eld slowly descended into the courtyard, his wingspan barely fitting within its confines. As soon as the huge wings ceased beating, Aenor was shoving her captive into the dragon-saddle and they were off.

Chapter 2

A enor was getting concerned. The Maester hadn't put up much of a fight at all. A mage of his power could have seriously damaged her by now. In fact, he was sitting quietly in front of her, trying to keep his wildly flapping robes intact.

Eld! Aenor communicated telepathically to her dragon. *What do you sense about him?*

He does not fight us, came a liquid gold voice in her head. *He is glad to be going.*

That's impossible! He was so worried about the Abida.

Eld shrugged mentally. *I only tell you what I sense.*

"Your pardon, my lord, for abducting you in this way, but I am willing to do anything to save my prince," she shouted against the rushing winds.

"No harm done Warrior, since you will be shortly taking me back home," he replied. Right on cue, the dragon made a wide sweep and started heading back to the cloister.

A wave of rage and pain from the dragon flooded her mind. *Aenor, stop him! He's in my mind!*

Aenor reacted, reaching forward to put Maester in a neck hold. She hadn't even managed to touch him when she felt his magic start battering at the protective amulet around her neck. It broke through faster than she thought possible and an excruciating pain exploded within her. She suddenly felt like she was being incinerated from the inside out. Struggling for air, she doubled over clutching her abdomen, all thought of stopping the man erased from her mind.

Firm hands reached for her then, keeping her in the saddle and easing the pain magically.

"Focus on your breathing, it will pass in a minute."

Aenor's breathing stabilized somewhat, the pain now receding amazingly fast. She took a couple of deep breaths to focus.

"Maester, it's clear to me that you were indulging me back at the college," said Aenor. "You could have stopped me right there, if you had wanted to. My question is: why didn't you?"

The Maester smiled wryly. "It was a nice diversion and I haven't been on dragon back for almost a century. They're not common here, you know. More importantly, I have to set an example for my apprentices. As you probably know, we're not allowed to attack, only to defend. I couldn't possibly have practiced that immobilization spell until we were well away from them."

"Wonderful." she ground out sarcastically. "I'm privileged to be your test subject." Her strength was suddenly restored by the thought of shoving him off the dragon. The Maester, on the other hand, casually began to study the vicious-looking sparks that started darting from one hand. Aenor stilled herself, thinking furiously.

Eld, if you have any control left at all, pretend to be in trouble.

Nothing happened. Aenor cursed silently. Then suddenly the dragon froze in mid-air, partially folding in his wings. They held in mid-air for a moment and then started dropping to the ground, tumbling head over tail. Both riders gasped in horror, but the Maester instantly closed his eyes and started muttering arcane words of magic to himself. Steadily, the dragon straightened out, borne up by the sheer strength of the Maester's will. Stealthily, Aenor began to unbuckle her thigh guard. As soon as she got it free, she lifted it high and brought it down hard on the man's skull. He slumped forward on the dragon's neck with a soft sigh. With the magic gone, they started dropping again. Aenor screamed Eld's name, and immediately lost the ornate guard overboard to take a firm hold on the unconscious man. The dragon quickly took over and righted himself about fifty feet off the ground.

Aenor was cold with fear. No matter how many times she had flown with Eld, no matter how much she trusted him, the sight of the ground spinning uncontrollably towards her had cracked her nerve. Getting stabbed in battle was infinitely better than getting splattered all over the ground like a bug.

Let's get as far as we can before darkness. The further away the Maester is from home, the less trouble he'll be, she instructed wearily as she adjusted her hold on the Maester. *I'll keep knocking him out until we make camp.*

Eld threaded his way through rocky mountain passes of the borderlands, finally reaching the verdant hills and valleys of Southern Norwall when the storm started brewing. Dark clouds seemed to appear from nowhere, boiling ominously around them. The mage was still out cold. Aenor had already sent him back into his unwilling slumber a second time.

Eld was uneasy. Even a dragon of his strength would tire very quickly against the buffeting winds of a major storm. But he also knew that time was of the essence. He would get his riders to Miramar, even if he had to fly through a hailstorm. He slowed his pace, conserving his energy for the battle ahead. That was when the other dragonriders appeared on the horizon.

I see them, Aenor answered grimly. *Their spies are better than we thought. Two of them, and a few griffons.* She loosened the battle lance strapped to the Eld's saddle. Lord Taren probably hadn't been able to spare more from his army but what he had sent was probably enough to keep the Maester from reaching the prince.

"Maester! Wake up!" she hissed into the man's ear as she started shaking him. He remained unresponsive. *Lovely! How the hell am I supposed to fight when I have an unconscious man to keep in the saddle?*

We'll have to land, Eld growled in response. The blood lust was rising in his eyes. He didn't want to expose himself to attack from the higher regions, but he also realized that the presence of the mage would keep his rider from fighting effectively. He dropped into a controlled dive, reaching the ground in a few seconds. Aenor unceremoniously shoved the mage out of the saddle and they were airborne again in the next minute.

Almost immediately, they were surrounded by snapping griffons, all darting in and out, claws extended to gouge out some unlucky flesh. Eld drew a deep breath and suddenly the world around them was red flame. Aenor winced from the heat, yanking out her battle lance from the harness behind her. When the smoke cleared, one of the griffons was plummeting to the ground with a shrill scream, plumage afire.

Eld went into a roll, heading after another griffon. A sharp set of claws gashed along his side, but a skilled thrust of Aenor's lance left a bright red splotch on the attacker's breast. It wouldn't live long. Almost immediately another set of claws fastened on her shoulder plates and yanked up furiously. Aenor felt some of her harness straps strain and then break. If the screaming beast kept on like this, she would be plucked out of the saddle and dropped like a stone to her death. Keeping hold of her lance with one hand, she reached for her short sword with her other and jabbed sharply upwards with it. A shrill cry from the eagle head, the claws dug deeper into her skin, another stab... and then another... blood flowing onto her hair, she screamed in fury and thrust. More blood and the lion's body dropped past her... fire everywhere... the smell of burnt feathers. And then, dragons.

The slower dragons finally arrived on the scene. Only one of the griffons remained to aid them, but the sheer magnificence of the green dragons did enough to dishearten their opponents. They circled lazily around Eld, their riders almost invisible on their broad backs.

Bad odds, Eld, Aenor telepathed.

Those dragons are slower than us. That's our advantage. Eld pivoted and soared up into the heavens. The two dragons exploded after them.

Eld made a swift loop and dived below one of the dragons, emitting a blast that singed its back. The other dragon immediately attacked from the side, flames heading straight for Aenor. She ducked, even as Eld dodged the blast adroitly. But then he screamed as sharp talons ripped into his flank, twisting around in mid-air to snarl and grapple with his attacker. Aenor lunged instinctively to drive her lance into the other dragon's side, putting her entire weight on its point. But the other rider had the same idea. Swiftly she deflected his lance with her sword, even as her lance sank into the shrieking dragon.

Just a little deeper, she panted to herself. The other rider produced a sword and hacked at her lance. *No time!* she shouted to Eld mentally, yanking the lance out to save it. Both dragons were locked together, wings flapping, mouths snarling, teeth and claws sinking into exposed flesh.

From behind, the other dragon attacked, air whistling as it hurtled towards the struggling dragons. Its rider held his lance steady, aiming straight for Eld's spine. Aenor heard the dragon's approach and twisted around to protect her mount but it was too late. The lance sank into Eld's flesh, snapping in two as the force of his attacker's dive carried its rider past them. Eld's scream of pain sliced through her, both mentally and physically. He started dropping towards the ground. Aenor cried out then, suffering together with her dragon, but sent a wave of her own energy to him through their bond.

The other dragons were coming after them. Eld kept dropping, the shock and pain freezing his muscles. *ELD!* she screamed in her mind, feeding him another surge of her energy. The huge wings opened slowly and caught the currents but they were still losing altitude. Eld slowly rolled into flight position as Aenor felt him recover. *Weak but alive!* Aenor felt her fury mount, churned it carefully and sent a surge of that to him. It awoke the battle lust in him again, as he swung up to face the oncoming dragons. Aenor swung her lance into position. *The left one!*

Eld shot up towards the left dragon, meeting its blast of fire with his own. Flames flowed over Aenor like water, bouncing off her armor but burning through the wool pants on her exposed thigh. Ignoring the pain, she used the cover of the flames to aim her lance directly at the oncoming dragon's breast. By the time the other rider saw her, it was too late. Eld's momentum drove it deep into the

17

dragon's heart. She let it go as they thundered past her, their screams fading as they dropped away. All Aenor heard after that was the explosion as the dragon hit the ground.

Pain. Aenor felt it. Her own and Eld's. She felt his exhaustion, his draining strength. She could feel his blood flowing around her from his back wound. She could feel the agony of her own burnt flesh. They could never survive an attack from the other dragon. She looked behind them to find it. *Diving? Diving towards the ground.... The Maester!*

Eld swung around to follow but his wing beats were faltering. He was losing too much blood too fast and he couldn't feel his back legs. *Dying.* The thought echoed in both their minds, but duty came first. They would have to defend the Maester. Carefully, he folded his wings in and dropped swiftly in a reckless dive.

The other dragon was sweeping along the valley where they had dumped the Maester, scanning for her victim. Seeing a splash of blue on the mountainside, she swooped in lower, working up a blast that would incinerate him instantly. She opened her mouth to blow, but her rider suddenly ordered a halt mentally. The robes were empty. Where was he? The dragon suddenly felt an insidious presence slipping into her mind. She bellowed, not recognizing it, but the force was too strong. She felt herself wheel around and head straight towards the cliff on her left.

The force of the blast tore away half of the mountaintop, sending an avalanche of rocks tumbling down into the valley.

Eld made an ungainly landing. Miraculously, he stayed on his feet for a minute before his bulk sagged to the ground. Aenor swiftly slipped off him to examine his injuries. The end of the broken lance was still stuck in his back and when she yanked it out, the deep hole started gushing a flood of black blood. She quickly grabbed some clean clothes out of her saddlebags and staunched the flow. Thinking swiftly, she calculated the time needed to stoke a fire and get her dagger ready to sear the wound closed. But blood spilled out with a speed that struck dread into her heart. Ruthlessly, Aenor forced her fear back down. Eld would need a clear mind to help him. He would not die.

Eld turned his head weakly to face her. Aenor gasped in horror. Part of his snout had melted under the flames from the other dragon. He had only one good eye left and it was regarding her sadly.

It's no use, came his golden voice in her mind. *The wound is mortal. My rear is paralyzed.*

"No!" she stormed. "This isn't over. We have the Maester!"

"I'm sorry," came a quiet voice from behind her. "I cannot help him. His spine is broken. Healing that is beyond my ability." He stepped forward to put a soothing hand on the dragon's neck. He turned his head slowly to look meaningfully at Aenor. "I can ease his pain though and make the end come much sooner."

Aenor paled and took a step away from him. *No, Eld. Please, I need you.*

She could feel the warmth radiate from Eld. *My friend, you know I love you but I can't continue like this. If my spine is*

19

broken, nothing will bring my legs back. Let me die as a fighting dragon, not a crippled one. I wish to be remembered as I was.

Aenor nodded slowly. She could understand pride and perhaps the proof of her love for him would be to let him go. She looked at the Maester. Her voice, when it came, was stark.

"Eld has chosen to die and it is my responsibility to see it done." The Maester nodded briefly, but compassion was in his eyes. He stepped back from Eld. Aenor walked over to the dragon's head. Bending over, she took one of the scales over his heart and broke it off. She looked at the iridescent scale for a long time before tucking in safely under her breastplate.

Lifting her hand over her shoulder, she grasped the hilt of the long sword strapped to her back and unsheathed it. The beautifully ornate design glinted softly in the dim light. She could feel the pain that the dragon was trying to hide from her. Peace descended when she finally accepted his decision.

Farewell, friend.

Goodbye dearest, she replied. Lifting a hand, she placed it on the soft, black nose of her dragon in farewell. His lone gold eye closed. Swiftly she placed the point of her sword against his breast and threw her weight on it. Eld stiffened, sighed softly once and it was over. Aenor withdrew her sword and let it slip from her hand. The two figures stood silently in respect as the oncoming storm slowly darkened the sky about them.

Eventually, the Maester moved forward to stand beside Aenor.

"Warrior, the storm will hit in a few minutes. We can shelter tonight under that ledge," said Maester, pointing to a rock outcropping on their left. Aenor nodded numbly. She knew that she should put together a survival pack from the contents of Eld's saddlebags but she just couldn't face doing that right now. Instead, she untied the food pack from his harness, made sure she had her weapons on her and started walking towards the small hollow in the hillside. The mage retrieved his robes, and followed her slowly, picking up fallen branches on his way.

Later, as firelight danced on the walls of the small cave, the Maester tended to Aenor's burnt thigh. She had shed her armor, leaving her in her brown wool flight jacket and pants. Red, blistered skin showed through her right pant leg where dragonfire had burned through to the skin. She winced as the Maester laid his hand on the ugly, puffed flesh. He closed his eyes then and took a deep breath. No chanting, no herbs, nothing. Aenor bit down on her lip as the pain intensified for a burning moment and then it faded as a sensation of coolness washed over her leg. He lifted his hand then, revealing a patch of redness where the burn had been. She stretched her muscles cautiously. No pain, just a feeling of tightness.

"Thank you, Maester. It feels fine." The Maester nodded in response, courteously turning away to forage in the food bag, giving her space to mourn.

There was only silence in Aenor's mind. For ten years, she had lived and slept with a dragon-shaped shadow in her mind. Even when each craved privacy, they were never truly alone and that comforted just as much as it irritated. It was only now, with the silence, did Aenor realize just how alone she really was. It took the trauma and pain of bonding to forge the chain between dragon and human and it was on her bonding night that she had realized that Eld would be her anchor in her new life. She had lost everything as a child and at eighteen; she got back a true companion. A tear spilled over and trickled down her cheek. She surreptitiously wiped it before the Maester saw.

Outside, lightning flashed as the rain started drumming on the rock overhang. The Maester handed her a piece of meat jerky. "We must be in Norwall by now," he began delicately. "You must know where the local garrisons are stationed. You can head towards the nearest one in the morning."

You can head towards the garrison. Singular. Aenor briefly shut her eyes. She had played her cards and there was nothing positive in the outcome. She was too numb to think through her options. For the moment, she just wanted to curl up and shut down. The Maester continued to regard her sympathetically.

"I'm sorry for your loss, warrior. Were you together long?"

"Ten years. He was supposed to outlive me." The pain in her words hung in the air between them.

"Let's get some rest. We'll sort things out in the morning."

Chapter 3

The next morning, the Maester shook Aenor awake. There was barely enough light for her to see him put his finger to his lips. Swiftly she came to her feet and mists of sleep began to clear. He was standing at the mouth of the overhang, looking out into the cold gray fog, his eyes focused and searching as if for something that only he could see. She came up beside him with her long sword drawn.

"There is power here," he said quietly. "Do you have a magic shield?" She nodded, fishing out a small pouch from beneath her breastplate. A twig cracked outside the cave. They both froze. Aenor could feel the presence now, all around them.

The Maester suddenly muttered a stream of unintelligible words and threw one hand upwards. Light exploded all around them, sending the shaggy creatures in front of them cringing away from the sudden heat. The fireball remained suspended in the air, flames shooting out to light their way.

Aenor yelled her battle challenge and lunged at the closest creature. It stood two feet taller than her, bound with muscle and brown fur. It also had the longest fangs she had ever seen.

Tamar, Aenor's aunt and a Queen's Guard, had once commented that the secret behind her niece's success in the Corp was due mostly to her speed and agility. She was certainly proved right as Aenor thrust her sword deep into creature's chest, ripped downwards and out, even as she dropped to her knees to avoid the blow the thing aimed at her. It let out a thin scream as razor sharp claws whistled over her head. She didn't wait to see it fall before she was attacking another.

Behind her, the Maester's chanting rose and fell, as shrieks and the smell of burning flesh reached her. Aenor didn't look back as she fought on, focusing on what she had to do. Suddenly light exploded around her as some force slammed into her body, knocking her to the ground. Looking up she caught a glimpse of swirling black robes before one of the creatures threw itself on her. She screamed as claws ripped into her body, as she struggled to find enough space to thrust her sword into its body. Suddenly the snarling beast stiffened and then collapsed on her. She barely heard the anxious voice and the hands pulling her out from under the creature.

Partially shielded by the Maester's body, she turned her head weakly in the direction that he was glaring. A dark mage stood there, black robes fluttering around him. Black eyes, black hair flowing down his back, he was an intimidating sight. He stood impassively for a second, as if making a decision, before making a courtly bow to the

Maester. The man holding her paused for a second, before acknowledging the courtesy with a nod of his head. As if on cue, a firedrake dropped from the sky and landed by the mage, who swiftly mounted and was gone in minutes.

"It's over," Maester said harshly. "For now." That's when Aenor passed out.

Aenor regained consciousness at mid-day. Her body throbbed unmercifully but instead of deep gashes all over her body, she found red, tender welts. There certainly were advantages to traveling with a healer. She sat up gingerly, wincing as recently mended muscles strained.

"Here, drink this." She took a cup of water from him. He too had been wounded, as the healing streaks across his body stood out clearly against his skin. She had been too groggy to realize it before, but the man had abandoned his robes and was bare-chested. With a sense of surprise, she looked him over discretely. She had sensed the lean strength of his body under his robes but she hadn't guessed just how well-made he was. In a single assessing glance, she had absorbed the sight of strong, broad shoulders tapering to a trim waist, well-muscled arms and legs that were displayed to their full advantage by the tailored breeches that he wore.

She was wary. Mages tended either towards flabbiness or scrawniness. It was pretty obvious that handling herbs wasn't the only exercise the Maester took. Swiftly she rifled through her memory for the legends surrounding him.

The Maester was once a Hurian mage whose unrelenting ambition had driven him to seek unending life. He had crossed into Norwell to apprentice himself to the first known Ageless: Margary. She was sketchy on the details but he had killed his teacher after learning her secrets and fled back into Huria to avoid the vengeance of her son. The real name of the son was lost in time, but he was known now as the Abida and he lived somewhere in the northern sanctions of Norwall. The legend stated that the Maester stayed well away from Norwell because he feared the Abida. It was never clear to her why the Abida didn't just bring the battle to the Maester in Huria, if he wanted revenge so much.

The Maester was Ageless not immortal, meaning that he could be killed like any human. He would not age as long as he could absorb energy from the living things around him. Ugly rumors abounded that he had lived so long because he had drained the life force of some of the sick who came to him for help. Alternate tales told of the Maester's regret, the rejection of his former ambitions and his desire to use his magic for the good of all. It was all a tangle of conflicting information.

"Those creatures. Were they sent by the Abida?" asked Aenor, as she got to her feet and stretched her sore body.

"Yes, but I wouldn't call that a serious attack. More of warning shot, a reminder that he's watching," he said with a flash of irritation, as he slashed his deep blue robes in the middle to render it hip length.

"You are very fast," he continued matter-of-factly. "I have rarely seen anyone dispatch those creatures as efficiently as you did." He cut off a long strip of material and used it to belt the shorter version of his healer's robe.

"Thank you, my lord."

The Maester turned his head to look at her. "I've decided to travel to Miramar with you."

That single sentence set Aenor back on her heels. She had figured that nothing could have made him consent after she had lost all leverage. She quickly found her voice.

"Thank you, my lord," her voice intense. "You have my country's gratitude. But what changed your mind?"

He smiled at her then. A smile of such utter deadliness that her relief shriveled within her and sent her mental defenses swinging back up again. This man was possibly a killer of hundreds.

"I've decided to remind the Abida how far I've come. There is a reason why he hasn't been able to touch me all these years."

There was clearly a story there but now wasn't the time to discuss it. Instead, Aenor reached down under her breastplate to pull forth a slim wooden rod from a hidden pocket on her flight jacket. "Astrid, our castle healer sent this for you."

The Maester broke the seal on it and drew forth the gossamer thin scroll. Unrolling it on the ground, he read the case description sent by his former student. Beside him,

Aenor pulled out a map and compass and began to plot the course to the nearest garrison, where there would be supplies and mounts.

Astrid was brief. Brandelein, the crown prince, had been injured in battle up north and taken home to recover. He had lay unconscious in his chamber while she and part of his guard stayed by his side. Astrid had just left for the kitchens to order food for the group, when Lord Taren's assassins had attacked. The guard had died to the last man, but they had taken the assassins with them. The last assassin had managed to slash the prince's throat before collapsing on top of him.

That was the carnage that had greeted the horrified healer's eyes as she returned to the prince's bedchamber with half of the castle in hot pursuit. With a great presence of mind, she had cast a sealing spell on the dying Prince and halted the gush of blood from his jugular. Unfortunately, the prince's spirit had already slipped away to the Darklands, even though his heart still beat in its rhythm. Going into the Darklands and bringing back a spirit was beyond Astrid's ability, so she begged her former teacher to come to her and perform the recovery. It generally took seven days for abandoned bodies to fail. Aenor had been travelling for a day so that gave the prince six days before the affinity between his spirit and body broke.

The Dragonrider's Quest

Aenor stood alone before Eld's body, praying to Mira silently. The dragon clans worshipped a dragon deity, but she figured that it wouldn't hurt Eld to have her goddess's favor as well. She placed her hand one last time on his heavy snout in farewell, before swinging a pack onto her shoulder. She had decided to leave her armor and lance, so she could travel light. Even the lightest alloy armor would feel like lead after a couple of hours. Her flight jacket and pants would suffice on the ground. She shifted the long sword strapped to her back, so that the hilt stuck up over her shoulder where she could draw it easily. Her short sword was buckled to her hip.

She turned away from Eld with finality and walked back to the cave, where the Maester waited for her. With a nod, he fell into step with her as they turned northeast towards the Southfeld garrison.

Chapter 4

The two companions traveled down the rocky hillside for an hour until the terrain flattened out. They had lost most of the day and had about a day's worth of food with them. With relief, they sighted some woods that would shield them from any airborne hunters. The woods were sparse and easy enough to navigate, with Aenor's compass keeping them headed in the right direction. The gods must have been on their side because they ran across a small, bubbling stream that addressed their water problem.

"This stream doesn't show up on the map. It must be too small," said Aenor, poring over the map that she had stashed in one of the pockets on her uniform. "It seems to flow towards the Southfeld garrison. There could be way-stations or hunting lodges along it that we can shelter in. Even if there aren't, we should be able to live off the land just fine."

The Maester nodded, looking pleased. Without further ado, they picked up the pace, weaving their way through the trees, keeping the stream on their left.

The Dragonrider's Quest

After the drama this morning, each lapsed into their own thoughts and turned inwards. The Maester, poring through the defense spells in his mind and Aenor thinking about Eld. Her lips curved as she remembered the aerial acrobatics that he was prone to when they were first bonded. Very flashy but utterly useless in a real fight. Eld had given up the theatrics when Lord Taren had rebelled and they were posted to the northern borders to fight in the war. Aenor's thoughts turned darker and her thoughts drifted to Taren's assassination attempt on the prince.

Brandelein. She had grown up with him. From the very beginning, the queen had noticed her speed and had singled her out to train as a junior member of the prince's personal guard. The prince had not been adverse to the fresh-faced girl, far from it. He had flirted outrageously with her, making her frighteningly aware of her own body. There had seemed to be a world of experience between his twenty years and her eighteen. She had yielded eagerly when he had taken her virginity one night, secretly and passionately.

Then the queen had found out and she was transferred to the Dragonrider Corps in the northern sanctions post-haste. There could be nothing between a prince of the royal house and a warrior maid. That was nine years ago and she'd been trying to get back into the royal guards since then.

The Maester returned to awareness slowly. He was satisfied that the spells he had dusted off would be enough to deal with whatever the Abida could throw at him. He cast a quick glance at his companion. She moved efficiently, but it was plain that her mind was far away.

Aenor cast a glance at the sky. The sun was already starting to set and they wouldn't get much further today. They had both been injured and the Maester had expended a lot of energy healing the both of them. Southfeld was a couple days' walk but there would be dragons or firedrakes there that would get them to the capital in time.

"Let's find a good campsite and stop for the night. We've both had a rough day and we can try to get an early start in the morning," said Aenor.

"Sounds good."

A loud snap sounded from behind her. Without thinking, she drew her short sword, pivoting around smoothly to protect the Maester's back. Her eyes met those of a placid piglet, snuffling happily at the base of a tree. She huffed in disgust.

A soft chuckle came from over her shoulder. "Our luck is holding. That's looks like dinner to me!"

Aenor stared uneasily at the piglet roasting over the small campfire. Her mind was racing. The kill was both the easiest and most terrifying she'd ever seen. She and the Maester had cornered the squealing piglet against a rock. All he did was lay his hands on it. The piglet went silent as its legs buckled and it slid down to the ground. Its eyes drifted shut and that was it. The whole thing had taken less than a minute.

She had not truly grasped, until that moment, the dangerous power that rested within her companion. The concept of such an ability resting in unjust hands shook her morality to the core. There were the rumors after all.

The Maester sliced into the piglet to check if it was done and expertly sliced off a hind leg and handed it to her. She took it silently, wondering if his magic had done anything strange to the meat. *Did he even eat?* Her answer came when he sliced off another leg and dug in with gusto, closing his eyes in contentment he took the first bite.

"I've just realized that I've been calling you warrior all this time. Given that we'll be traveling together for a time, we should probably introduce ourselves properly. My name is Marius."

"Aenor Merivel," she responded, after she swallowed a bite.

"Aenor. Unusual name. Is it a family name?"

"Not that I know of. I think my aunt would have mentioned it, if it were."

He shot her a quizzical look. "Your aunt?"

"My parents were killed when I was seven." Killed was a very kind word for it. "My aunt took me in. She was a dragonrider too although she's grounded now."

"I'm sorry that you lost your parents so young. Your childhood must have been tough."

She shrugged, uncomfortable but trying to appear nonchalant. "My aunt took good care of me. As soon as I was military age, I volunteered and the rest is history." Aenor then flipped the topic around, a long-time defensive maneuver to keep people from digging too deep.

"What about yourself? I've heard some stories but some of them sound so fantastic that they discredit themselves."

"What do you want to know?"

Aenor paused for a second, considering how best to ask the questions racing through her mind. *So do you drain your patients on a regular basis? How often exactly? How soon will you need another top-off?*

"Tell me about how you killed that piglet?" she asked instead.

"Well, you've probably heard that I absorb energy from living things. I've learned to control the rate. Most of the time, I draw energy from the plants and trees around me, but I can also do it from animals."

"And humans?"

"Yes, humans as well. It would be more accurate to describe me as an energy exchanger. I can store energy, push it out as well as absorb. That's how I heal. I feed enough energy to accelerate the body's ability to heal itself. That's why I couldn't heal your dragon's spine. If an injury is such that the body cannot heal itself, I cannot force it to do so."

Silence reigned for a moment and then he continued.

"You've probably also heard that I've drained patients to prolong my own life," he stated bluntly. Her eyes flew up to meet his. "Yes, I have done so. Not to prolong my life but to end their misery, and only at the patient's request. It is a terrible mercy and the families don't always accept their loved one's decision."

"That must be a difficult situation to be in," she said quietly, unsure if she could believe him. She hesitated a moment before delicately proceeding. "Have you ever used the power in anger?"

He looked her directly in the eye as he answered.

"Yes. In my early years my control was erratic, especially when I became emotional. And I was very emotional and damaged in those early years after I got back from Norwall." He looked away to gaze into the flames. "I wore gloves to protect those around me, but accidents did happen. A dear friend and mentor was bedridden for days after one such accident."

"Was that person called Margary?" Aenor probed further.

"No, it was Maester Martel, the Maester of the college at that time. A very good man. I had made it over the mountains and he offered me rest and help in training my new abilities. Maester Martel recognized my potential in healing and worked with me to perfect my control. I had no interest in healing at that time so I left to try my luck as a battle mage. I spent the next thirty years travelling as a mercenary. When I heard that the Maester's health was failing, I returned with my wife to say goodbye and wound up staying to learn the healing arts," Marius concluded simply.

"Your wife?" asked Aenor, thoroughly surprised. A wife didn't fit with the stories she had heard about him.

"I was married with two children," replied Marius, a slight note of pride in his voice. "My wife's name was Iris and we were together until she passed away. My son Donal's line died out a hundred years ago during a border war, but Fern's descendants are merchants in a nearby city. We do keep in touch but it's awkward between us. It's difficult for them to reconcile that I'm a living ancestor," he finished quietly.

"I'm sorry," she replied automatically, still struggling with the concept of an Ageless being a family man. "You must have some ability at mind control as well. You were able to control Eld yesterday."

"I can control animal minds for short periods. Humans are much more conscious about will and boundaries and thus can enforce limits more effectively. I can't enter human minds unless I'm invited in, so you needn't worry about your privacy." Aenor felt a flicker of relief but could she really trust the Maester to tell her the truth about a skill like that?

"So you were at the college for three hundred years, something like that?"

Marius grimaced. "It sounds rather grim when you say it like that, but yes. I travel around but usually find my way back there. I started teaching about two hundred years ago and eventually became the Maester. Truthfully, being around young people has kept me energized. Not literally of course," he said with a twinkle. Aenor cracked a smile at that.

Marius rinsed his hands with water from the water bag. "I'm worn out. I think I'll turn in." With a goodnight nod, Marius pulled the robes tighter around himself and lay down facing the fire, closing his eyes.

"Good-night." Aenor sat up for a few more minutes, mulling the information that she had gathered about her travelling companion. Eventually, she pulled the end of her braid forward to untie it and drew her fingers through her hair until it rippled about her in tight waves. She pulled a lock forward meditatively and regarded it. Her hair was her single rebellion and concession to vanity. She could not bear the thought of hacking it off, even though it would give an opponent one less handhold. Flipping the lock back over her shoulder, she proceeded to unsnap the fastening down the length of her jacket. She loosened the laces of the linen bodice she wore under the jacket and then settled down on the ground for sleep.

Chapter 5

It was already light when Aenor awoke. She sat up slowly, scanning the campsite. The Maester was gone but his pack lay a few feet away. A couple of hard cakes sat roasting on a flat rock set in the embers of the fire. He was probably washing at the stream, which sounded like a good idea to her. Aenor sniffed an underarm. Yes, a wash was definitely required and more importantly, it would clear her head.

Aenor moved through the trees until she emerged at the cheerful stream from the day before. The Maester sat on the riverbank, pulling on his boots. He had clearly had a morning swim as his hair was wet and his robes stuck to him in places.

"Good morning, my lord," she said, her voice still scratchy from sleep. She crouched down to scoop up a sip of water.

"Good morning," he replied. "The water's fairly cold but it's clean. Breakfast should be ready when you're done."

He got to his feet, dusted himself and headed back to the campsite.

Aenor stripped all the way down and slid into the water, gasping at the chill. The stream was only about waist deep but that was more than enough for her needs. She scrubbed herself as fast as she could, before climbing back out into the warmer air. Hastily, she rubbed herself dry with her jacket and got dressed.

Back at the campsite, the Maester (it would take her a while to think of him as Marius) handed her a roasted hard cake. The roasting had sadly done little to improve its flavor. They didn't have much food left and she didn't have her bow with her, so they would definitely need to ration. At least water wasn't a problem. After dowsing the fire, they proceeded back with their journey.

Last night's meal and information exchange had eased them both and they chatted randomly about the situation in Norwall as they travelled. There years earlier, Taren, the hereditary lord of the north, had rebelled against the royal family and essentially tried to succeed from Norwall. So far, the rebellion had been restricted to the north of the country and the royal forces had been successful in establishing a line and pushing the rebels back, inch by painful inch.

"So were all the dragonriders sent up north?" asked the Maester.

"Most of us. Some pairs are rotated back to Miramar every year to defend the capital. Eld and I rotated back about six months ago and have been on scout duty and perimeter defense." Aenor swallowed a pang when she spoke of Eld.

40

"How bad is it up there?"

Aenor shook her head. "It's taken a long time but we've got Taren boxed in the mountains. The problem is that the mountains are his home ground and his people know how to defend their territory. It's become more of a guerilla war than anything else. One of the northern dragon clans is backing him, so he pretty much knows where we are at any given time."

"So it's likely that he's going to come looking for us again?"

"Possibly. He can't know yet that his dragonriders are down. But he'll figure it out when they don't return, probably by the end of today. He has fewer dragons than we do, so the loss of two will be a blow to him. I doubt that he'll risk sending more dragons to hunt down two people when he needs them to defend his own lands."

"Then it's likely that all we'll be dealing with is the Abida."

Aenor nodded. "He struck much quicker than I expected. You said that was more of a warning shot?"

"I think so. He knows by now that I'm continuing to move north. It's just a matter of time before he strikes again and, next time, he won't hold back. Unlike Taren, he doesn't need to see us to know where we are."

After a couple of hours walking, Aenor spied a small farmhouse in a pretty meadow right outside the tree line. A few chickens pecked between the neat rows of vegetables and a woman was hanging her washing out on the lines strung out between two fruit trees. Aenor fished through her jacket pockets for coins and came up with a silver and a gold. After some inspired haggling, they left victoriously with some cherries, a few boiled eggs and a plucked chicken. Things were definitely looking up and, if they kept up the pace, they would be in the capital in plenty of time.

That night, after they had roasted the chicken over the fire, Aenor considered the man reclining opposite her. The Maester had kept up easily with the punishing pace that she had set that day. His longer stride probably made it easy for him, but it was clear that he was used to physical activity. His work at the cloister probably did keep him running around, but she was still impressed that he kept up without complaint. He didn't feel the need to chatter on, which was a great relief since she tended to stay on the quiet side. She still struggled with reconciling the man with the legend, but the fact that he hadn't tried to drain her yet spoke in his favor.

"So tell me about yourself," Marius said. Aenor came to with a start.

"There's not much to say really. I am twenty-eight years old, only child of a merchant and a mage. They died when I was seven and my Aunt Tamar raised me from that point on. I enrolled in warrior training at sixteen and here I am!"

"I like a succinct story as much as anyone, but surely you could expand a little on that." Aenor cracked a smile at that.

"My family has this tradition. One person from every generation enters the Guards. Tamar was the one from her generation and I am the one from mine. I was never intended to be an only child, but that's the way it wound up. I have one cousin on my mother's side but that's it. Tamar never had children so I suppose it's up to me to keep the name alive. I was intending to have a child when I get grounded. Assuming that I live that long."

"No prospective father on the horizon?"

Aenor shrugged. "Not at the moment and I'm not ready for all that anyway. I want to get further in my career before I consider a husband or a child."

"It's good that you know what you want."

"What about yourself?" she asked with curiosity. "What is it that you want out of your life now? You've already experienced more than the average person."

"I've had an interesting life, to be sure," Marius replied ruefully. "It took me a while but I eventually figured out that I preferred growing things to killing them off. This may sound strange to young ears but I am content being a teacher and healer. Chasing power is not all that it's cracked up to be."

Aenor considered inquiring about the Margary legend but decided to leave it. She was now satisfied that he posed no immediate danger to her or the prince. They would only be together for a couple more days, so she didn't see the point of digging further into his past. He would be part of her past soon enough.

Chapter 6

A enor shifted restlessly all through the night. She dreamed of her mother, walking with her through a strangely white garden with manicured shrubs here and there. She popped awake in the morning, with a leaden head, trying to recall what her mother had been telling her.

She sat up slowly, feeling a little off. She looked towards the sounds of splashing from the stream but couldn't see much as the bank, on which she lay, sat at a higher level than the actual stream. She got to her feet, peering down the slope to see the Maester floating on his back, totally nude. That wasn't the problem. She had bunked in barracks most of her adult life where prudishness couldn't survive. The problem was that the moment she clapped eyes on him, a familiar warmth started to uncoil deep within her. A purposeful yearning.

Oh no, no, no. Not now!

Marius flipped to his feet, dunked himself under the surface one last time and waded to the bank, completely oblivious of her gaze. Water cascaded lovingly down the length of his body, practically in slow motion. Her eyes glued themselves to his chest and then slid lower. Her body approved. A lot. Warmth turned into heat as the urge to mate began to rise.

Aenor squeezed her eyes tight and stood motionless on the bank, absorbing the horror of the moment. She was nowhere near the time for her onset. Then a flicker of hope awoke. If this was a normal physical reaction to an attractive man, the water would help. She stripped down to her skin swiftly and waded into the stream. Cold water closed over her head, the sudden shock to her system shutting down her burgeoning arousal. She stayed down for a minute, before popping back to the surface, gasping for air but grateful for the reprieve. After a quick cleansing, she dried off and clambered up the bank back to the campsite, feeling a lot better.

Marius was crouching over the food pack, still only half-dressed. Aenor swung her eyes away from the sight, her hands balling into fists as she concentrated on keeping her thoughts from straying. *Gods, this can't be happening. Not for another year!*

"Walk and eat, Aenor?" Marius called out.

"Sure," came her muffled voice and as she bent to pick up her pack. When she walked towards him, her face was controlled but pale. He handed her a boiled egg. "Is something wrong?" he asked sharply.

"No, nothing," she replied with a brittle smile. "We've got a full travel day ahead, so let's make the most of it." *Please, please put your robe back on,* she begged silently.

Marius shrugged into his robes and raked his hands through his wet hair to comb it. He swung on his pack. "Ready?" At her nod, he kicked soil onto the embers at this feet and started off into the trees. She swore furiously in an undertone, setting off after him. *Really? Is this one of your jokes, Mira? Can you make my life any worse right now?*

After several hours, Aenor was walking in an electric aura generated by her hormones. There was no doubt in her mind now that her onset had hit early. She was burning up and exhausted, fighting both herself and the terrain. The feeling of the linen small-clothes she wore, rubbing against the swollen, wet flesh between her thighs was agonizing.

Marius settled into a comfortable stride, ahead of her. Aenor's eyes were fixed determinedly to the ground in front of her, but an image of his bare back lived in her mind. The broadness of his chest, tapering down to a narrow waist and firm, muscled buttocks. The fire flared again in her groin. She bit a finger savagely to douse it. The sharpness of the pain cleared her mind a little. Temporary relief from the urges that would only get stronger.

She could withstand this. *I will withstand this,* she swore determined. The idea of being caught in the throes of a sexual frenzy was impossible. In the middle of nowhere, with no protection, a child would be inevitable. She pressed a hand against the ache in her lower back. The painkiller powder she had taken didn't seem to work against something like this. *Mira! You bitch!* She swore in a fury. *You have no right to do this to me!*

Marius stopped so suddenly that she walked right into him and tripped. He caught her and steadied them both. Aenor gasped softly and stiffened. Her entire body seemed to focus on the touch of his hands on her upper arms. Marius frowned.

"Something's wrong. You're burning up."

"It's been a tough day. I'm just tired," she said brusquely

He tilted her face up to examine it. Sizzling green eyes met silver gray ones, which widened as her pheromones began to surround him, and arouse him, just as they were intended to do.

"Aenor," he whispered.

"Damn it!" she yelled, pushing him away. Her frustration finally found a release in a sudden fury. "Leave me alone!" she sent a kick towards his shin.

"Calm down!" he yelled right back at her, grabbing her arm and spinning her around to put her in an arm lock. Aenor could only whimper as her length of her body came against the length of his.

"Gods," he groaned as her bottom pressed suggestively against his groin. "Aenor, why the hell did they send you out to me if you were due for your onset?"

"They didn't. I'm not due for another year! I have NO idea why this is happening now," she moaned, as she squirmed against him.

Marius winced as the combination of pheromones and her squirming set his penis swelling.

"All right. I'm going to let go of you now and we're going to deal with this."

Aenor folded to the ground as soon as he let go of her. Her body was trembling like an autumn leaf, but she was too humiliated to care.

"Let me help you," said Marius urgently, crouching down beside her.

Aenor lifted her eyes to meet the sight of the straining bulge in his breeches. "No," she said in a strangled whisper. "If this really is the onset, I would get pregnant for sure. I don't have a potion and I bet you don't either."

"Unfortunately, I didn't have the contents of my stillroom on me when you kidnapped me!" he snapped, struggling to keep his wits. The blood was draining from his brain to his lower half, responding biologically to the scent of a woman in heat. He reached for his control and backed away from her to put some range between them. *Think, think, think.*

'There's got to be arbouria here somewhere, probably near the stream. In fact, cool off in the stream while I look. It should slow the progress somewhat."

She nodded. "All right."

"I'll be right back," he promised, as he headed off to the stream to hunt for arbouria. Aenor just flopped back on the ground and groaned up at the sky.

Marius was having no luck at all. Rockwort, glansa, every useless weed in the world grew on the stream bank but not arbouria. No arbouria, no potion, no protection. He ranged further in the woods, but the likelihood of finding the herb was less there as it was too shady. He emerged back at the stream to find Aenor lying back in the water in her smallclothes, her linen bodice and shorts rippling gently in the current. Her eyes opened as soon as she heard his muffled steps.

"No luck yet. We'll keep our eyes open." He plopped down on the stream bank. Submerged as she was in the water, he was spared her scent. Aenor was very nicely built, but she didn't welcome his attentions and he wasn't entranced with her either. He grimaced. So sexual frustration would just have to be a major part of his life for the next few days. Creating a child with a woman he'd just met just seemed like the height of irresponsibility. And Maesters were never irresponsible.

"I'm sorry for losing control back there," she said sincerely from the water. "I have no idea why my onset is hitting now, but we can't afford to waste time dealing with it. We have to keep moving while it's still light. I can manage this and it's going to be easier now that you know. We'll just keep a little distance between us."

He gave her a level look. "I admire your optimism, if not your sense of reality."

"Look, you don't know me," she retorted. "If I say that I can do it, I *will* do it." She stood up, the water cascading down her body, plastering the near-transparent linen to her skin. She stuffed her uniform in to the pack, yanked her boots on and swung her pack to her shoulder. "Let's get moving." She marched off, choosing to let her underclothes air-dry and cool her for a while.

An hour later, Aenor was struggling. Two hours later, she was in the abyss. The Maester stayed several feet behind her, out of range of her scent but close enough to keep an eye on her condition. He got whiffs of her scent here and there, but it was manageable. Aenor swerved to head back to the stream, dropping her pack on the bank and wading in full dressed. She plunked down in the water and leant back until she was submerged. She surfaced a minute late with a splutter.

The shock of the water had calmed her down somewhat. The urge had faded into a faint throb in the back of her consciousness, but she knew from experience that this would only be a momentary reprieve. She gritted her teeth. They were losing too much time because of her and her frequent stops.

The same thought was running through the Maester's mind as he rested on the stream bank, waiting for Aenor to emerge. Cold water helped but it didn't address the root of the problem: the biological imperative of the onset. Clearly, it was possible for women to endure it without having sex. Nuns managed, although he didn't really want to think about how.

Aenor stood back up and sloshed to her pack. After wiping her hands dry on the pack, she withdrew her map and sat down a few feet away from him. "This says that there should be a supply station about three hours from here," said Aenor, after studying her map and compass. "It's unmanned but there should be emergency rations and water." Even as she spoke, she could feel the urge stir within her. Three hours suddenly seemed like forever. Without wasting any more time, she repacked efficiently and got to her feet. Marius put a gentle hand on her shoulder.

"How do you feel?" Her body immediately turned towards his touch. Aenor flushed, looking away in embarrassment.

"Not bad," she replied awkwardly. "We really should get going before my sex drive decides to come back on." He nodded, a little warmth coming into his eyes. "You're doing amazingly well, you know." She smiled back at him, appreciating his encouragement. Without another word, they headed away from the stream towards the supply station.

Four hours later, after a few wrong turns in the dark, a crudely built cabin loomed up within the lighted circle cast by their torch. Aenor was sweating profusely, her face flushed in the soft golden glow as she fought against the most basic of impulses. The door unlatched easily under her hands and creaked open to reveal the cabin's dusty interior. Both packs fell to the floor and the door slammed shut behind them, as Aenor found a lantern on a shelf and began to crank the handle to charge up the cell. A dim light appeared and brightened steadily as she continued to crank, outlining the dust and the dilapidated condition of the cabin. There was a roughly hewn table pushed up against a wall, a bench and a folding camp bed in the corner. Marius went around the small room, opening the windows to let some fresh air in.

"I'll go look for some wood," he said stepping out the door. After the lantern was fully charged, Aenor started going through the cupboards and found a small gold mine of supplies. Everything from dried jerky, biscuits and hardcakes to blankets, towels and soap. Delighted with the turn of their luck, she stuffed a small piece of jerky in her mouth and chewed devotedly as she started to restock their packs.

Marius ducked back into the hut with a few pieces of wood. "There's a stack of firewood and a well on the side of the hut. Somebody left this place well stocked."

Aenor handed him a strip of jerky. "Here. This will take the edge off. I need to cool off again." She grabbed a towel and ducked out of out the hut as Marius got on with building the fire. Instead of heading to the well, Aenor walked a short distance into the woods to take care of her problem in private.

A little later, Aenor was feeling a lot better as she poured buckets of well water over her nude body, sluicing away the dirt and perspiration. She reveled in the sheer pleasure of cleanliness and the weight of the water flowing through her loose hair. Night had settled heavily on the land but the light streaming out of the cabin's open windows colored her lithe body with a loving hand. Marius caught a glimpse of her through a window and glanced away as his body started to react again.

Aenor squeezed the water out of her hair, smiling to herself. A hard climax, a bath and a little food in her stomach had stabilized her mood. Even with all the stops, they were actually making decent time. It would be another day's walk to Southfeld at the minimum. For now though, she looked forward to more food and a few hours of sleep. Grabbing a thin towel, she dried herself off efficiently and wrapped herself in it. She scooped up her cleansed uniforms off the well and headed back to the cabin to get warm.

He met her at the door, turning sideways to allow her by before continuing on to have his own bath. Aenor dragged the lone bench over to the fire and draped her clothes over it to dry. With a sigh, she straightened up, glanced out the window and ran into the sight of Marius shaving his face in the nude. This time, she didn't look away.

She absorbed the deep scar that ran the length of one muscled thigh. And that his lower body was a work of art. Unconsciously, she began to repeat recent history and watched him at his bath. She watched the deliberate movements of his hands with the razor, drew in her breath in appreciation when he stretched to draw another bucket of well water. She smiled when she heard him yelp as the coldness of the water hit his skin and she stared fascinated as the water flowed through his hair and down his body.

And when he sensed her gaze and gray eyes met green, she allowed her eyes to tell him that she found him attractive. He lifted an eyebrow charmingly, gesturing down as if to say 'this is yours if you want it'. She shook her head firmly and turned away, but the smile didn't leave her eyes or her lips.

Chapter 7

Aenor awoke with a start, propping herself on the camp bed with an elbow. For the first time in days, she felt rested. Even as she made the realization, an inexplicable unease set in. She rose and swiftly shrugged into her driest uniform, all the while trying to figure out why the back of her neck was prickling uncomfortably. After her short sword was safely on her hip, she strode over to the door and pushed. It held true. Frowning, she put her shoulder to it and shoved. The door didn't even shift.

"Maester," she yelled. "I'm locked in!" It was then she noticed the unearthly silence that enveloped her. No bird song, a truly unusual occurrence for this time of year. She darted to a window and tried it. It was sealed too. She put her eye to the crack between the edges of the peeling wood and peered out. All she could see was a hazy blue film overlapping the well in the distance. She yelled for Marius again at the top of her lungs. When no answer came, her unease deepened into a certainty of danger.

Daphne Ignatius

She threw herself against the door, her shoulder making a sickening thud as it made contact with the rotting wood. A corner of the door broke off from the rest and hit the floor. She dropped to one knee to break off more from the area when she stiffened in surprise. In the space where the chunk had been was a pulsing pale blue film that shifted and glowed with a life of its own. The Abida had made another move. She slid a finger through the space, cautiously feeling the film give a little before suddenly firming up and pushing her finger back into the cabin. Dread settled around her heart. The door and windows were sealed against escape. She put her hand to the magic shield slung around her neck. It was obviously not enough to overcome the field. Then an idea hit her.

With a focused yell, she threw a sidekick at a part of the wall. The sound of splintering wood echoed through the cabin. Another kick and another, while portions of the wall cracked and fell apart. Eagerly, she peered through the crack that had formed. Grass grew a few inches away, glowing a bright green in the morning sunlight. She grinned in triumph before swinging back to her feet and resuming the pounding. As the wall shuddered, cracked and splintered she sped up, ignoring the pain as she alternated legs. Suddenly her right foot went right through the wall and three minutes later, she scrambled through the shattered wall out into the light. Behind her, the blue film still pulsed around the exit points of the cabin

"Maester!" The cry rang out into the deathly silence, as she quickly scanned her surroundings. Then suddenly, she felt a soft touch on her shoulder. She swung around, settling into a defensive stance. There was nothing there. Then again, a faint pulling. Uncertain, she drew away from

57

whatever was there. Another tug, a little more insistent. "Oh Mira!" she swore, before sprinting in the direction the tugging was leading her.

As she shoved her way through the thicket, she caught a whiff of burning wood. When finally, she crashed into another clearing, the smell was overpowering. Her mind froze as it tried to absorb the extent of the destruction before her. In the middle of the flaming clearing, two figures struggled in a full-scale mage duel.

Bolts of blue fire flashed between outstretched hands, glancing off protective shields before falling in a shower of sparks around the pair. There was not a single living thing within a twenty-foot radius around them. At the other side of the clearing, sounds of falling branches reached her as a forest fire took hold. Then suddenly, Marius caught sight of her and gasped. His opponent took his momentary advantage and cast a fireball at Marius, which knocked him back, his shield pulsing erratically as it tried to keep up with the pounding.

The black mage sneaked a quick glance at Aenor to judge her position. She dropped into a side roll as a flash of blue lightning struck the bushes where she had formerly been. Quickly, she scrambled back into the relative safety of the thicket, wisely realizing that she would only be a hindrance instead of help in this fight. With her out of the way, the black mage turned back to his original prey, who had staggered back to his feet. Both mages had burns slashing across their bodies, their clothes smoking from the impact. Once again, they started circling each other, constantly muttering, softly weaving spells to confound, disrupt and destroy each other.

Suddenly, Marius shouted something and stretched out one hand. A tree branch came whistling straight at the black mage's head, but he ducked just in time to avoid being brained. The ground at the Maester's feet suddenly heaved and opened up, throwing Marius to one side. He lithely curled up into a roll and came up to his feet swiftly before returning a punishing blow of mage fire at his opponent. It hit the magic shield squarely, causing a ripple over its invisible surface as the shield weakened. Another blow in the same spot and the dark mage staggered back, his ornately embroidered black robes swishing about his ankles. In front of him, Marius was a distinct contrast in his ragged half-robe but he stood firm, ignoring the pain of his wounds and forcing himself to conserve his strength.

They circled each other, ancient words weaving the substance of earth and air into deadly weapons. The elements came at their beckoning. First lightning and hail to weaken, then fire to wound. And with each phenomenal display, they were killing themselves. The black mage's face was drawn, his cheeks hollowing themselves out until it resembled a skull. Marius moved like an old man, struggling to keep his balance but the power that moved around him surged and trembled with strength. Two forces that were perfectly matched. And then there was a shift in the balance.

From overhead, a fierce scream cut through the smoke. From out of the black smoke billowing above the clearing, a large dark shape hurtled towards Marius, wings spread out to the max. Deadly claws sliced right through his shield and ripped into his face and shoulders. Marius dropped to his knees with an agonized scream. Aenor gasped. Unfair! She took off, drawing her short sword as

59

she sprinted towards the two figures. The black mage let loose a fire bolt which slammed into Marius, knocking him into an awkward sprawl a few meters away. His body twitched once and subsided into unconsciousness.

The black mage turned and caught sight of Aenor running toward him. His eyes rested on her for a brief moment before he raised his hand dismissively. With another blood-curdling scream, the firedrake returned at its master's command, this time zooming in on Aenor. She twisted to avoid its deadly claws, dropping to a roll to come to her feet, ready for the next attack. The black mage, satisfied that she was going to be busy for a little while, walked cautiously to where Marius lay among the jagged, smoldering ruins of what had once been a meadow. Fire crackled from his hands and he kicked the motionless body viciously. Behind him, the firedrake dropped out of the sky again, streaking down on its victim. The black mage smiled, the last thing he did. Marius's eyes flew open, his hand struck out and the mage bolt that emerged ripped right into the black mage's heart.

Aenor heard the shrill scream but she had problems of her own. Talons raked into her shoulders, sharp teeth snapping at her face. Steel swung and was rewarded by a scream of fury. A brown firedrake rose above her a few feet, blood dripping from a shallow gash in its side, hissing angrily. Without warning, it dropped on her again, knocking her on her back, exposing her dangerously to its claws. She kicked to push the flapping, screaming creature away from her and then sprang to her feet, using her momentum to channel force into her swing. The sword sliced into the firedrake's neck, sending a spray of ichor outwards over her. The shocked beast crashed into her, pining her down amid struggling limbs and flapping wings. Hot ichor burned Aenor's skin as she struggled, gasping, out from under the creature. She came to her feet, looking over at the two silent bodies lying amid the destruction.

She rolled the black mage's body unceremoniously off Marius and swore violently. Her hand searched for his heart, and a faint fluttering rewarded her for it. Suddenly he started hacking, blood spilling from his lips. Aenor swore and shifted him gently onto his side to prevent him from choking as series of spasms racked his body. After the attacks had passed, the Maester's eyes drew open slowly, his gaze unfocused. Aenor bent down closer to him.

"Maester, do you know me?" she asked gently. He nodded and then jerked as another fit of coughing took him.

"Tell me how to help you," she urged. "What should I do?" His eyes flew to her face as his burnt hand groped for hers.

"Life-force. I need it," he whispered, his voice dry and crackling. "Will you give?" Aenor froze for a split second but then her resolution firmed.

"Take whatever you need."

Aenor closed her eyes and willed her strength to him. She felt something pull deep inside her, getting stronger and stronger until it started moving to their joined hands. It didn't hurt a bit but her self-preservations mechanisms kicked in, urging her to jerk away. As strength drained slowly from her body, her mind started swimming and her body began to tremble. Her eyes flew open; her gaze fearful even as Marius's grip on her hands tightened and he drew on her life force. Aenor bit her lip as her body started to shake violently and darkness began to descend, but she didn't allow herself to break away. By then, it didn't matter anyway because she crumpled to the ground in a faint.

Aenor came to, the blood pounding in her head. She was lying beside Marius, still amidst the destruction. She moved cautiously. As far as she could tell, she was fine. Drained but fine. She inched towards Marius slowly. He looked more like a man dead than alive. Terrible burns marked his hands and body while dark, clotted gashes slashed across his face and shoulders. But beyond all that, his breathing was even and his heartbeat steady. Aenor breathed a quick thanks to Mira, as she shook him awake gently.

"Aenor," he croaked after a few tries. "Are you all right?" She nodded hastily.

"We need to get away from here now." She looked around them. "We're too visible." The smoking, blackened ruins around would serve as a banner especially when seen from the sky. Marius winced as he tried to move. His body was a single scream of agony but even that was distanced by the sheer sense of relief that he was still intact.

"I can barely move. You'll have to help me. But first, I'll need to gain more strength. From a tree, I think," he amended as he sensed her reluctance to donate more. "Help me to a strong oak."

Three trees later, he was sleeping like the dead, as his body started to rebuild itself at an inhuman rate.

Chapter 8

Aenor was feeling really low. The Maester had been badly hurt and they had lost another half day. She had just trapped a small rabbit in the woods for their next meal, but the thought that they were not going to make it in time to the capital was foremost in her mind. As she traipsed back through the wood with the rabbit slung over her shoulder she allowed herself the luxury of brooding over all the mistakes she had made during this journey. *If only I had seen the lance heading towards Eld,* she castigated herself bitterly as she put one hand onto the shack's door and pushed it open. *If only I had…* She gasped. The rabbit fell to the floor as she swung into an attack stance.

The young man standing over the sleeping Maester had turned swiftly on the sound of the door opening and gaped at her obviously practiced moves. He put his palms up in the internationally recognized signal of peace. "I mean no harm," he said quickly.

"Get away from him," demanded Aenor. He complied quickly. Aenor circled around to put herself between him and the prone healer. "Now, tell me who you are."

"I'm the ranger for this sanction. I saw signs of a forest fire from the air and I came down to investigate. I was checking out the damage to the hut when I noticed this man." He suddenly caught a whiff of Aenor's scent, which had intensified due to her agitation. His eyes widened as he realized what that signified. His gaze unconsciously dropped to the Maester's body as he instinctively sized him up. "Pardon me for intruding," he continued self-consciously, as a faint blush colored his cheeks. Aenor ignored his discomfort. She had bigger problems.

"How did you get here?" she asked guardedly. She had learnt from the past that powerful people of all kinds used youthful and innocent-looking people as their best weapons.

"Firedrake," said the young man, gesturing towards the outside.

"Show me."

Tied to a tree behind the shack lurked a dun-colored, very real firedrake. It showed its yellow teeth and hissed as Aenor and the man approached it.

"He's not a very friendly fellow," said the man, still struggling with the embarrassment of the situation and his involuntary reaction to a woman in the middle of onset.

"I can see that," replied Aenor dryly, as the animal snapped at them both. Her mind raced with the possibilities. Hope loomed on the horizon. She fumbled with the seal of the Imperial Guard tucked away in one of the hidden pockets of her uniform.

"I need your mount," said Aenor, as she handed it to him. The young man's eyes widened and grew more confused as he absorbed the import of the seal. "I'll send back a patrol for you once I get to Southfeld." Her voice lowered as she deliberately took on a confidential tone. "I'm on the queen's business."

"Of course. Anything I can do to help you, warrior," stammered the young man, handing back the seal to Aenor. He was immediately graced with a dazzling smile.

"What is your name anyway?" asked Aenor belatedly.

"Andrei," he replied shyly, as he became the recipient of another flashing smile. "Thank you, Andrei," she said sincerely.

Thirty minutes later, Aenor helped a shaky Marius into the firedrake's saddle. Andrei was holding the head of the beast steady but he really didn't have to because the animal had become a lot friendlier after he had gotten a whiff of Aenor. Apparently even some animals related to the pheromones a woman emitted.

When they were ready, she lifted a hand to wave to Andrei. He nodded and smiled back at her. The firedrake crouched down low to get the thrust it needed to get off the ground. A jerk and a sudden thrust of the wings and they were airborne and back on their way. Sitting behind her, Marius leaned up against her back and instantly reentered his healing sleep.

Heading due north, Aenor calculated the time needed to reach Southfeld. They would reach there just before sunset, which meant an entire day lost. However, there would be a squadron posted there and fresh mounts. And the potion she needed. She smiled softly. They had finally gotten a break.

The Maester awoke with a start. For the first time in hours, his mind was clear and functioning. He took swift inventory of himself. His burns and cuts had healed well; everything seemed to be functioning normally. Next he took stock of his surroundings. Aenor and he were airborne again. His mind had dimly registered the breaks they had made to rest the laboring firedrake. Aenor turned her head to glance at him.

"Feeling better?"

"Yes," he yelled back over the rush of the wind. "How are you doing?"

"Good." But she was blatantly lying. The urge had hit once again while he was out. She had been straining against it for a couple of hours now.

The Maester's gaze rested on the back of her flight jacket. It was soaked through, a reliable signal. He didn't have to ask to know that she was struggling, but he also knew that he was far too weak to do anything about it.

Chapter 9

The firedrake circled over the Southfeld garrison and then swooped down, responding willingly to the touch on its reins. In a clatter of claws and a cloud of dust, they landed in the courtyard. A young guardsman ran up to take charge of the firedrake. Aenor and the Maester announced themselves as they dismounted and were escorted to the captain's offices.

Dia Assemate, captain of the Southfeld garrison strode into the office and took her seat behind a plain desk. A wide swath of gray cut through her hair, but her manner and her obvious health made her look like a woman half her age. With a smile and gesture, she invited them to sit. Aenor swiftly outlined their mission, unwillingly noticing the slight furrow in her hostess's brow as she gazed at the younger warrior woman.

"Maester, we are honored by your presence. Please accept the services of our healer for anything you desire."

"That's very kind of you," he replied smoothly. "I am sore, in need of a large meal and sleep."

"Of course." The captain rapped on her desk. A young guard entered and was instructed to guide the Maester to the healer's wing. As Aenor stood to accompany them, the captain gestured her to a halt. Marius cast the captain a questioning look, but bowed to the both of them and then turned to leave with his escort. Aenor sank slowly back into her chair and turned to face the captain.

"Aenor Merivel," started the captain without preamble. "What are you doing here during your onset?"

"It started quite unexpectedly after I picked up the Maester," replied Aenor baldly. The concern in the captain's eyes was understandable.

"Were you prepared?" she asked bluntly. Aenor shook her head. A hiss of breath escaped the captain's lips and her eyes involuntarily flicked down to her midsection.

"Then you are-" Aenor cut her off quickly.

"No, there is no way I am pregnant. I've… been taking care of the situation myself," Aenor stated, as she colored in embarrassment. The captain relaxed.

"That is a relief. I hate to see a young warrior's career cut short by such an incident but there is no need to deny yourself further. We have several good partners here for you. Feel free to select whomever you wish. Our healer will make sure you are supplied with the prevention potion and anything else you need."

"Thank you, Captain. The Maester and I need to continue onwards as soon as possible. I would like to request two fresh firedrakes or a dragon if you have one, and I'd like to leave as soon as the Maester is rested." The furrow reentered the captain's brow.

"Don't worry about that, Aenor. I'll have another warrior escort him to Miramar."

"It's my mission to fulfill," stated Aenor flatly.

The captain nodded in resignation. "As you wish. Please see the healer before you leave. She will be able to provide you with whatever you need. We will have the firedrakes ready for you in the morning."

Aenor clattered down the stairs of the barrack, turned the corner and promptly bumped into a broad chest clad in armor.

"Aenor!" came a delighted voice from above her.

"Embry!" she replied happily and hugged him. An old buddy from a couple of years ago, Embry was one of the most charming men she had ever known. Predictably, he caught the scent of the onset as it swirled upwards towards him.

"Aenor," he said in concern, as he moved her back to look into her eyes. "What are you doing here *now*?" Aenor sighed as she repeated her story for what appeared to be the tenth time. And all during her tale, she watched the hunter enter his eyes as his body responded to hers. After she was done, he swept her into his arms and claimed her lips in a proper hello. When they parted again, her cheeks were flushed and her breath came in swift pants. Lust had once again reared its demanding head and found him very, very suitable.

"Aenor, we been friends for several years and I respect you both as a warrior and a woman. More than that, I care for you. I would take care of your needs in…." he continued on, selling his skills in that particular arena. Aenor didn't hear much of it as her attention had already been captured by his other attributes. Her gaze swept down his body eagerly. Long and lean, with sunlight streaks in his hair, Embry was a very attractive man and it was clear from the bulge in his breeches, that he was ready to get going.

"Thank you, Embry," she said in an agonized voice. "You must know that I want to desperately, but I'm to leave in a few hours."

"That's more than enough time," he whispered seductively to her. She groaned in frustration. *Gods!* Embry was perfect for her. She liked him. He would pleasure her into senselessness. The mere thought of their bodies moving together sent washes of driving need though her. *Maybe, if I find the healer really, really fast.*

Embry felt her resolve waver and swiftly stepped into the breach. She found herself pressed up against the wall of the corridor, his lips on her neck and his hands coming up to rest temptingly under her breasts. A warm, wet tongue swept up from her shoulder to her ear, making her yelp from the stab of pleasure that shot straight to her groin.

"But if you're sure you don't want me…" came a low, sensuous voice in her ear as his body pressed into hers. Aenor bit back a groan.

"Embry, I really have to leave in the morning," she said, catching his face between her hands. "You need to make sure that I do." Embry chuckled.

"No, listen to me! I have to get the Maester to Miramar tomorrow, and my will… My will may be weak."

Embry sobered up at the serious look on Aenor's face. He nodded at her. "I swear that you will depart in the morning, even if I have to tie you into the saddle myself," he answered.

Aenor relaxed at his words, the last of her resistance crumbling into dust. *I need this. Time to get to the healer!*

Chapter 10

Fed and refreshed after a memorable night, Aenor thundered down the stairs towards the courtyard. The Maester was waiting beside a pair of firedrakes, looking particularly inscrutable. Aenor was a tad easier to figure out because she was glowing like a candle. She flashed him an optimistic grin as she tucked the precious vials of prevention potion into the creature's saddlebags. They both swung into their saddles. As Aenor gathered up the reins in her hands, her eyes lifted to meet a pair of laughing blue eyes looking at her from a top floor window. Embry was leaning, bare-chested and grinning, against the window jam, arm lifted in a jaunty salute. With an answering grin and wave, Aenor took to the skies with the Maester right behind her.

Four hours later, Aenor's stomach was starting to rumble. The landscape beneath them has changed into the pastoral meadows of central Norwall. The silver glint of a small lake appeared on the horizon. Their mounts would need to be watered and fed. Aenor looked over to the mage gliding besides her with a meaningful look. He nodded in reply. A slight pressure with her heels and her mount responded by circling down. She guided the firedrake to the lake, flying low over the rippling water before drawing to a landing on the lake edge. Marius landed with a thump beside her a minute later.

A half-hour later, the site was the epitome of domesticity, with lunch spread out on a blanket and two hungry firedrakes gorging on tough chunks of meat. The Maester was lying in the sun, in much the same position she'd first seen him, eyes closed, drawing energy from the ground beneath him. Aenor tossed the animals the remainder of the meat they had picked up at Southfeld. Traveling with firedrakes had its disadvantages. They ate a lot and had already finished off all the meat from their restocked saddlebags. But they were also tough animals and would get them to Miramar this evening. Unless yet another incident occurred.

Behind her, Marius rose to his feet and moved to the blanket to eat. When she returned to the blanket, he handed her a savory chunk of rosemary bread. She folded down beside him, taking an occasional bite of the bread as she stared at the lake meditatively. She was wonderfully calm and relaxed and she knew why. Aenor smiled to herself softly. It had been good to see Embry again.

Beside her, the Maester ate quietly, not looking at her at all. Of course he knew what had happened. He'd have to be blind not to. His ego warred with his reason. Of course, he knew what she had done was perfectly acceptable and rational. Unmarried women often took the opportunity of trying out different lovers during the onset, all the better to determine compatibility for the normal times. In all honesty, he was a physical wreck from the duel and wasn't up to the challenge. Even with all that rationale, it stung that she had chosen to share herself with another.

An hour later, they were back in the air and Aenor was finally letting herself get excited. By her estimation, they were only one or two hours away from Miramar. *We're going to make it!* And that's when she caught sight of the dots on the horizon to her left.

She squinted her eyes against the sunlight, trying to make them out and the direction in which they were flying. *Two fliers. Could be a patrol since we're close to the capitol. If Eld were here, we would know for sure.* A little wary, she kept an eye on the dots as they continued on. But then the dots started growing larger.

Alarms going off in her head, Aenor assessed their situation swiftly. She only had her swords and no lance. Firedrakes were no match for either dragons or griffins. Outrunning their pursuers was the smartest option.

Aenor waved and yelled to catch the Maester's attention. The wind stole most of her voice but the Maester must have noticed the motion because he looked back over his shoulder at her. She pointed to their distant pursuers. He squinted and saw them. Glancing back at her, he nodded to confirm that he saw them. Aenor pointed to their firedrakes and then pointed forward. She spurred her firedrake to go faster by snapping its reins. It snarled in complaint, as it was still sluggish from its earlier meal, but complied. On her right, the Maester did the same.

Aenor hunched forward to reduce air resistance and glanced over her shoulder as her firedrake shot forward. The dread in her heart grew. The distance between them and their hunters continued to steadily narrow but she was now fairly certain now that their pursuers were not mounted on dragons. They were too small.

If only you were here, Eld, she murmured to the empty corner in her mind. Riders could only communicate telepathically to their bondmates, but dragons were not as restricted. He could have called for help from the dragons at Miramar. Out of frustration, Aenor slammed her fist on the pommel of her saddle and screamed mentally. *WE NEED HELP HERE! CAN ANYBODY HEAR ME?* Silence. Aenor swore, hunched back up and grimly spurred her firedrake on.

Firedrakes are marathoners, not sprinters, thought Aenor. *Our mounts won't be able to keep up this pace for long. The Maester is still weak and he'll need to conserve his strength for the prince.* The answer was clear. She would have to turn and face their hunters, in order to buy time for the Maester to get to Miramar. It was a flawed plan. She would be hard-pressed to keep both hunters away from the Maester. Thinking through possible battle tactics, Aenor failed to notice the string of dragons rising from the mountain range on her right.

Marius glanced back towards Aenor and then shifted his gaze further back, to their hunters. They're catching up, he thought grimly. Sunlight flashed off armor and he thought he saw feathers. *Griffins. Wonderful.* Aenor's face was set as she bent low over her beast, urging it along. His firedrake was starting to labor under the pace. *We're not going to make it.* His grim thought was answered by a bellow from his right. Marius whipped his head around to the other side to see what new horror had been laid at their doorstep.

A flight of three dragons hurtled towards them. Behind him, Aenor bolted upright as she gaped at the dragons that had apparently manifested from nowhere. *Young dragons. Riderless. Friend or Foe?*

The flight split, two dragons shooting past them, heading straight for their pursuers. The third dragon slowed and banked, soaring gracefully over them to take the lead. Aenor looked over her shoulder just in time to see their pursuers veer and turn tail. Two griffins were no match for two dragons, even immature ones.

In front of her, the lead dragon dipped down to settle itself at their level. The two firedrakes knew exactly how to react. They separated, maneuvering to get behind the dragon's wingtips to catch its slipstream. Aenor felt her firedrake relax in relief, its wing beats slowing as it drafted along in the dragon's slipstream.

Behind her, the remaining dragons returned and settled behind them to guard their rear. Where had they come from? Her eyes turned to the mountains on their right. The Silver Claw warren? Aenor turned to look back at the nearest dragon. It was a blue dragon, well-built but probably too young to have a bondmate. Its golden eyes flicked towards her curiously, but then focused straight ahead again.

Hello? Aenor telepathed tentatively. *Can you hear me?* The young dragon didn't even twitch an eyelid as it powered forward, ignoring her. Aenor turned forward, mind roiling in confusion as she tried to figure out what had just happened. *Thank you Mira! This had to have been your work.*

Aenor caught a movement on her right and looked at Marius to see him making a questioning gesture. She mimed confusion and shrugged in an exaggerated fashion. Then she stiffened as her gaze went past the Maester. A relieved grin split her face, as she pointed towards the spires of Miramar that had just appeared over the horizon.

Chapter 11

The guards at the royal palace of Miramar spotted their company at a distance. Aerial patrols swept towards them for verification. Aenor flashed them her seal. A few minutes later, the two firedrakes landed under heavy guard while their dragon escorts sailed overhead and then banked to head home. Identities were verified, introductions were made and a formal escort formed to lead the pair straight to the Healer's quarters.

'Maester!" The castle healer hurried forth to meet the procession. "Thank Mira, you are finally here! Gods, what happened to your face?"

"Astrid!" the Maester clasped her outstretched hands in his own, smiling down at her even as he deflected her questions. "You look… terrible."

"This has been a terrible time," sighed Astrid. "I'm so glad that you're here. You both should know that the Hurian ambassador was here three days ago, breathing fire." Aenor grimaced. "He's threatening a diplomatic incident over your extraction." Aenor's eyebrows raised slightly. Extraction sounded a lot better than kidnapping. "The queen assured him that you were safe but none of us knew for real until we got the bird from Southfeld this morning."

"I'll take care of the ambassador," stated the Maester firmly. "Clearly, I'm in one piece and none the worse for wear." Astrid looked relieved and then turned to Aenor and smiled encouragingly.

"Warrior, we're all grateful for what you have done. Don't worry about repercussions. You're a hero in many books, including mine."

Gods! Aenor thought. *I certainly hope so. 'Caused international incident' doesn't look good on one's record.*

"You must be starving." The Maester shook his head firmly.

"No, please take me to the patient." Astrid inclined her head in doubtful acceptance but escorted the Maester and Aenor to the prince.

Aenor gasped as the sight of her prince. Brandelein looked quite dead. No breath lifted his chest, his face was chalky and the bandage around his neck was clean except for a thin line of red where his wound had bled slowly through. The Maester sat on the side of the bed. Taking a deep breath, he placed his hands over the prince's and closed his eyes slowly. Swiftly, he performed a cursory inspection of Brandelein's injuries.

As the Maester visualized the prince's body in his mind, healthy tissue shimmered with a faint blue light, damaged areas with a deep glowing red. He focused in on the traumatized region of the prince's neck, checking over the damage carefully. It looked like a work of art, he acknowledged to himself. Astrid had grown far beyond the skills he had taught her as a student. Blood vessels had been stitched painstakingly together with silk, tissues brushed with the juice of the tisra plant, before being sewn up. Marius swiftly checked over the rest of the prince's injuries. Nothing major. All that was required now was the return of the prince's life-force to animate this shell and start up the healing process.

Marius opened his eyes and removed his hands from the prince's, looking encouraged.

"Everything looks good," he said, looking over at the castle healer. "You've done wonderful work."

Astrid inclined her head, accepting the compliment modestly. "I've sent word to the queen. She should be here shortly. In the meantime, please accept some refreshments," As Astrid turned, she nearly bumped in Aenor who was still haunting the room.

"Perhaps warrior, you would like to rest?" hinted the healer gently, catching the faint scent of the onset. Aenor flushed faintly.

"Thank you, but I think I should stay here awhile longer. The Abida has attacked twice so far." The healer shot a glance back at her former Maester.

"Yes, perhaps that would be best," he smiled. "I don't think I'll be much use right now if anything untoward suddenly happened."

At that moment, a commotion sounded in the outer rooms. A second later, the queen's retinue entered into the prince's chamber.

"My lord!" The queen swept forward in a swish of heavy silks to take the Maester's hands. "Thank Mira, you are finally here!"

"Your Majesty," replied Marius, bowing smoothly. "It is a pleasure to be able to serve you and the prince." The queen looked over at Aenor and then glanced questioning at the Maester as she too caught the faint scent. Aenor colored a little, but plastered a stoic look on her face, knowing that she had done nothing to be ashamed of.

"Dragonrider Merivel. My thanks to you for getting the Maester here safely," she said as she held out her hands. Aenor sank onto one knee, and kissed the fingers of both hands in the royal salute.

"It was a fairly uneventful journey, Your Majesty," smiled Aenor faintly. The smile on the queen's face broadened.

"I'm sure it was..." she replied. At a single look, another warrior stepped out of the retinue. "Tamar, you should thank Mira for your niece's safe return."

Marius took in Aenor's famed aunt. She was almost an exact copy of the niece, except that her hair was cropped and waved about her face charmingly. In her, Marius could see Aenor in twenty or thirty years. Tamar, in her turn, folded her niece in a tight hug.

"Majesty, it is no surprise to me that Aenor is back here, hale and hearty. She has the uncommon luck of the insane." Tamar pretended to cuff the younger warrior affectionately. She was rewarded instantly with a flippant grin.

The queen then moved to her son's bedside to stroke his hair gently. The smile on her face faded into a look of loving concern, as she looked down at the pale face of her only child.

"Is there hope, my lord?" she asked softly.

"Of course, Majesty. He is young and strong, and the castle healer has done a sterling job in setting up his recovery. All I require now is some incense and perhaps your help." The queen swung around to meet his gaze.

"Anything!" she swore intensely. "What do you desire of me?"

"I will need an anchor when I travel to recover your son's life-force. Someone with a vested interest in his successful return. Both our lives will depend on that person. We will not make it back otherwise."

"Of course, my lord! Instruct me in what I should do."

Tamar stepped forward immediately. "A moment, Majesty." She turned to face the Maester. "How dangerous is this position of 'anchor', my lord?" she asked sternly.

"There is an element of danger involved," answered Marius plainly. "The anchor serves as exactly that, an anchor in space and a guiding point in the Darklands. He or she would also serve as an energy reserve for me, should I drain myself too far. If things go badly, the anchor risks being pulled into the spirit world along with me and the prince."

"Then you are saying that there is a chance that the queen could be lost, as well as the prince?" she pressed.

"Yes," replied Marius, matter-of-factly.

Tamar shook her head. "Then it is impossible. The queen cannot take that risk," she stated firmly. The queen started to protest before being quelled by her bodyguard's stern gaze.

"Majesty, think of the possible consequences! Both you and the prince out of reach. The country will be thrown in chaos and we will all be under Taren's thumb in no time at all. As your guard, I cannot allow it."

At that point, the hereto ignored Aenor stepped forward.

"I can do it," she announced. Tamar sent her a questioning look.

"I have a vested interest in getting the prince back safely. I have already put my life at risk to get the Maester here." *And Brandelein was my first lover,* she added silently. Looking over at the queen's face, she could see that the other woman remembered that too.

"You've already done enough, Aenor," began Tamar, her protective instincts kicking in. "I should be the one. Plus, you're not... yourself." At that point, both the Maester and the queen overruled her.

"I know and trust Aenor, whereas I don't know you," said the Maester firmly to Tamar, putting an end to the argument. "Aenor would work better for my purpose." Every gaze in the room turned onto Aenor, standing with straight spine, looking wonderfully confident on the outside but busy quailing on the inside. Being lost forever in the Darklands wasn't a particular pleasant prospect. But a warrior's duty was to take risks like this for her liege lord.

The queen clapped her hands, startling everybody in the room. "Everybody out! Astrid, bring incense immediately." She turned towards the Maester, taking his hands once again.

"My lord. Please bring my son back safely."

He nodded. "With your prayers, Majesty."

An hour later, with the scent of the incense to relax him, Marius prepared to slip into a meditative trance. Aenor and he sat side-by-side on a comfortable bench beside the prince's bed. Marius reached forward to pull the prince's limp hand towards him, settled back and picked up Aenor's hand as well. Aenor had been put into a half-trance by the

Maester minutes earlier, awake enough only to be aware of her surroundings and of what she had to do. Marius closed his eyes and focused on his breathing.

A few moments later, Marius found himself floating gently within his own mind. Slowly, he willed himself upright even though position was just an illusion in this dimension. Everything around him was a distracting whirl of rose and purple but there was actually order and beauty in the patterns. Slowly, he turned to see the shadowy image of Aenor over his shoulder. She sat there immobile, more like a cardboard cutout than a three-dimensional being. At her throat pulsed a silver glow, the heart of her life-force. He reached for it and drew a thin thread of light from it. Swiftly he tied it around his ankle, using her as a lifeline. His way home. When he was ready, he concentrated his energy and drew a long rectangle before him with his hands.

The faint outline of a doorway appeared before him, its edges wavering. Beyond that, the Darklands, the realm of thought and belief. Swiftly, he shifted into his favorite avatar, a peregrine falcon, mentally imbuing himself with a falcon's speed and exceptional sight. With a challenging shriek, he drove through the portal and into the shifting mists of the Darklands.

Wings outspread, he shot through the dizzying patterns, the trail of light streaming from his clawed foot. His eagle eyes searched before him, looking for a similar trail, anything to show him where the prince existed. Every now and then, small explosions of lights occurred around him as other souls entered and departed the Darklands almost instantly on their way to Mira's arms. Suddenly, he noticed a faint trail, turned dark with age and broken up but certainly showing the presence of a being. Swooping down, he lined himself up with it and shot further and further into the unknown. Flashes of images and voices came to him as he traveled, none of which he recognized. Then suddenly he slammed through a painfully hard wall.

Trilling in surprise, he spread his wings and landed onto a firm floor. Around him was the semblance of a peasant's hut and sitting at a corner table was a little dark-haired boy. Marius transformed himself back into his human form as fast as he could. When he rose to his feet, the boy was looking at him disconsolately. Marius gasped at the familiar face. Faint memories suddenly crystallized. A peasant woman with a young boy laid out on an examining table. The faint words "Please my lord, bring back my son." He had failed to find the boy then but fate had allowed it this time. *If only, it wasn't a century too late...*

"Do you know where my mama is?" asked the boy hopefully a high, piping voice. Marius regarded him, searching for the words. The child had been here alone for over a century, not knowing what had happened to him. Waiting endlessly for his mother to return home. Guilt and the horror of the situation suddenly overwhelmed him. *Did I look hard enough the last time?* This child had paid the price of his failure. Marius shook his head in mute denial. *Marooned here all alone...*

A soft tug on his robes brought him back to this reality. The small face looked hopefully up at him.

"Do you know when she'll be back?"

Marius sank onto one knee, struggling to regain his composure. The small face in front of him looked into his eyes trustingly. He felt another wrenching bolt in his soul. *This is inhuman!* Every moment he sacrificed to help this child lessened the chances of his finding the prince but every single fiber of his being demanded that he correct this situation. He took a deep breath.

"Your mama had gone to Mira's arms, child, and she wants you to meet her there." At the puzzled look on the boy's face, he continued quickly. "Don't worry about a thing, I'll help you get to her."

His mind raced. It was obvious that the boy did not know what had happened to him and that he had, by sheer force of will, kept himself here waiting for his mother. *How am I supposed to get this child to go onwards when he probably didn't even know what death and heaven is?*

The only way he could start a change was to convince the boy to go into the unknown. To be willing to face it alone. And what was a better symbol of going out into the unknown than walking out the front door.

"What is your name, young man?" he asked.

"Jenest, sir."

"Jenest, your mother is waiting for you in another place, a better place." Marius forced a smile to his lips. It's like a big festival there, with all sorts of goodies and kids to play with!" Jenest perked up at that. "Wouldn't you like to go find her there?"

Jenest looked a little uncomfortable at that. "Mama said that I can't go out by myself. She told me to stay here until she got back. She would be real angry if I showed up there without permission."

"Well, she got delayed," replied Marius, improvising skillfully. "She told me that she was worried that you were here all alone and I told her that I would give you a message when I came through here. She wants you to walk there and it's only a very short walk at that."

"Can't you come with me?" asked the boy plaintively.

"No, son," replied Marius gently. "It isn't time for me to go there yet. But a brave boy like you needn't worry about going by yourself." Marius took Jenest by the hand and drew him to the door. This was the point where things could fall apart.

"Don't be afraid by what you see," he said softly as he opened the door. Beyond the doorway was the terrifying chaos of the Darklands. The boy shrank against him wordlessly as he looked out into nothingness. Marius got back down onto his knees to look into the boy's eyes.

"Remember Jenest, your mama would never let anything happen to you," he said gently. "Nothing out there can harm you. Just trust in her and yourself..." With that he planted a swift kiss on the boy's forehead. "May Mira take care of you."

Jenest turned to look at the darkness before him and took the first step to eternal rest. And another. And disappeared in a flash of light. Marius shut his eyes against the brightness. The floor beneath him disappeared, as did the rest of the cottage. It was time for him to move on.

He was a falcon again, flying through nothingness, searching for his quarry's trail. He didn't know how long he had been flying and it didn't really matter. Here in this realm, he had the strength to fly forever. Suddenly, he caught a faint whiff of humanity and then he saw it, a faint trail of light in the darkness. Once again, he swooped down to follow it, his own light trail blazing brightly behind him. The end of his search was upon him in moments.

Prince Brandelein sat in a shadowy copy of his bedchamber, reading a book. He lifted his head off his knees to see an unusually large falcon land beside him on the seat of an empty chair. He knew exactly where he was so it didn't surprise him in the least when the falcon's body unfolded into a man, sitting beside him.

"His Royal Highness, I presume," stated the stranger, somewhat stylishly.

"Who are you?" demanded Brandelein.

"My name is Marius. Your mother sent me to bring you back."

Brandelein's lips curved into a bitter smile in response. "Is there much of my body left over there?"

Marius looked somewhat startled. "Your body is perfectly fine."

"Are you lying?" asked the prince, a challenging glint in his eye. "I have no wish to go back and find myself a cripple or worse."

Marius took a chair by the prince. This certainly wasn't what he had expected. He ran a hand through his hair meditatively.

"I swear to you on my honor, that the only injury you sustained was a slit throat, which has been expertly healed," he said wearily. "The truth is that even if you go back, there is no guarantee that your body would let you in. At that point, you would have the choice to move on or stay in this realm." The prince remained silent.

"I can't force you to go back with me, of course. But personally speaking, I would grab any chance, no matter how faint, to get out of this place. There are a lot more appealing choices than spending eternity here."

The prince cracked a smile. "I was beginning to get a little bored," he answered wryly, tilting his imaginary book to reveal its blank pages. Lifting his head, he took a long look at the emptiness around him. "Shall we go?"

In the prince's chamber, deep night had fallen and the two figures near the bed remained frozen in trance state. Around them, sat the faithful few watching for a change. Any change. Tamar stood stoically behind the queen's

91

chair. The castle healer had fallen asleep from energy drain in a chair. The queen herself looked like a cold, marble statue as her eyes stayed on her son.

"Selene." The Queen started at the low voice and looked over her shoulder.

"Selene, go to bed. I'll keep watch for you," said Tamar kindly. The queen shook her head mutely and turned her gaze back to her son's silent form. Another moment passed in silence. And then the body in the bed jerked spastically, as it drew in a shuddering breath. The queen sat up in her chair and uttered a hopeful cry. The prince drew in another long breath. The queen was out of her chair instantly and bending over him, calling his name. Tamar sprang forward to wake Astrid who leapt to the prince's side, checking his pulse and the bandage around his neck carefully.

An instant later, Marius uttered a groan and opened his eyes slowly to witness pandemonium erupting around him. Warriors running out the door to spread the word, the queen weeping openly over her son, the healer trying to convince everyone to back off and give the prince some air. Behind him, a soft moan as Aenor came back to herself, aching in body and spirit, feeling completely strung out. Marius smiled a soft, beautiful smile to himself, sank back into his chair and dropped into a deep, healing sleep.

Chapter 12

One week later

All welcome the Maester of the Hurian college of Healing Arts!" echoed the chamberlain's strident tones through the vast hall. Aenor kept an appropriately respectful expression on her face, stifling a snicker at the pretentiousness.

Marius strode through the tall, gilded doors of the Receiving Hall, richly embroidered blue velvet swishing about his heels. At the end of the long carpeted walk, sat the queen in her royal robes, glowing like a rich jewel under the sparkling lights overhead and smiling at him in welcome. As he walked down the rows of dignitaries, he recognized the Hurian ambassador and bowed his head as he passed. The Hurian ambassador looked smugly pleased, mollified now that Norwall was publically recognizing Huria's part in saving its royal heir. As Marius approached the dais, he started searching the crowds subtly for a familiar face. He found it.

She was standing in the ranks of warriors close to the queen. Strawberry blonde hair flowing loose for once about her shoulders, dressed in silver mail rather than armor. She met his gaze with her own, and flashed him a conspiratorial smile. Suddenly, he was heartily wishing that he didn't have to go through this ceremony. Memories of flying free through the skies with a self-reliant woman suddenly seemed a lot more appealing. But when the queen stood up, walked towards him and took his hands in hers, he reacted smoothly and perfectly. Raising his head after kissing her hands in a royal greeting, she surprised him by kissing him gracefully on both cheeks.

Smiling warmly at him, her voice rang out like a clarion in the silent hall. "This is the healer that gave us back our prince!"

The jubilant cheering shivered the chandeliers shining overhead. The cheering died slowly away as the queen gestured for silence. "At this moment, the heir is recovering well and busy trying to empty his warrior's purses in a game of dice!" Laughter spread like music through the hall.

"And we owe it to you," she added slowly, looking straight into the Maester's eyes.

"You do me great honor, Your Majesty. It was an honor to be of use to Norwall. May the friendship between our two countries grow ever deeper." The Queen nodded, her violet eyes deepening momentarily.

"Dragonrider Merivel!" Aenor stepped forward smartly, her boots ringing on the polished floor of the chamber as she walked forward to stand beside Marius.

"You brought the Maester to us safely and at great peril to your life," she stated clearly. "In all ways, you acted nobly and…" *Sure,* thought Aenor. *Kidnapping the Maester was a real noble gesture.* She finished the thought just in time to hear the queen's last words.

"It is our desire that you fill one of the vacant positions on the Prince's Guards. Do you consent?" Aenor gasped in shock. Behind her, a congratulatory murmur rank through the ranks of the warriors behind her. She had expected the queen to offer her a post in her own guards, not the prince's.

Aenor finally found her voice. There were much worse things than to be part of the future king's guards! "Your Majesty, it would be an honor!" The queen nodded with a smile.

"Your Majesty," came a quiet voice from the Maester. The queen turned to face him gracefully. "I have a request for you regarding Dragonrider Merivel." She gestured for him to continue.

"I have decided to seek out the Ageless known as the Abida." Aenor turned disbelieving eyes on him.

"Why?" asked the queen. "Isn't he a danger to you personally?"

The Maester nodded. "That is precisely why I wish to seek him out. He has become… inconvenient. I intend to find him and challenge him to a duel. It is time for this matter to be put to rest."

Whispers flooded the silence. The queen and Aenor exchanged surprised looks.

"I'll need someone to watch my back and I can think of nobody more suitable that this warrior," continued the Maester. He turned to face Aenor.

"Dragonrider Merivel, will you join me?" he asked, his eyes clear and direct. Every eye in the room turned towards the silent figure of the newly elevated warrior.

The sound of whirring wings grew in the room. Suddenly, glass shattered all around them. Dagger sharp shards started dropping in deadly falls from the high windows. Thousands of birds swarmed into the room in a flurry of deadly claws and beaks. Every warrior there reacted instantly. Tamar leapt upon the queen, bearing her to the floor and covering her with her own body.

"To arms!" shouted Aenor at the top of her lungs as she reached over her shoulder to draw her sword. Behind her came the hiss of steel as the Queen's Guard closed in around their liege. She heard a muffled yelp from Tamar as the queen dug an elbow into her guard's stomach and shoved her off. Aenor cast a swift look over her shoulder, protecting her eyes with one arm. She saw the Queen's rich robes fall to reveal a simple white chemise and a jeweled sword strapped to her hips. Her face was impassive as she drew her sword to join her warriors.

The screaming started as everybody in the hall scrambled to get out. The doors swung open as the crowd streamed relentlessly through them, effectively preventing the guards outside from shoving their way in. The birds swooped and dived all through the hall, attacking indiscriminately with beaks and talons. Then out of the dark mass of shrieking avians came three figures, walking forwards calmly. Two black mages and a figure dressed magnificently in scarlet and green.

"Lord Taren sends his regards," said the scarlet mage calmly, as he held forth his hand. A mage bolt hurtled towards the cluster of warriors. Aenor cried out in fury as she saw the two warriors in front crumple to the floor, their flesh sizzling. Then out of nowhere, Marius leapt in front of the remaining warriors, eyes blazing as he swept out his hands to form a shield. All three mages lifted their hands to fire simultaneously. Aenor didn't wait to see more. She dived quickly behind the protections of Marius's shield as the guard rushed the queen out the doors behind them. The mage bolts struck. She heard the Maester cry out in pain as he deflected as much of the energy as he could. Blue light rippled around his shield, making it visible and showing clearly where the bolt had broken through. The scarlet mage in the middle laughed tersely, bowed to his comrades and dematerialized in a shimmering mass.

"Go!" hissed the Maester without looking back at Aenor. At that moment, the guards from outside finally struggled their way into the hall, screaming their war cry. Both the remaining mages turned at the sound involuntarily. That was all the chance Aenor needed. She grabbed the dagger hidden in her boot, stepped out from behind the shield and threw it, all in a smooth fluid motion. The female mage turned just in time to see death coming, as she took the silver blade into her throat. She toppled to the ground with a horrible gurgle. Marius laughed, a rather dark sound, as he blasted the remaining mage with a stream of magefire. The dark mage brought up his shield just in time to protect himself, but it was already over for him. There was no way to win against both the guards and the Maester. Aenor grabbed Marius's sleeve.

"Let them take care of him," she yelled. "We've got to get the other one." They turned in unison as the stream of guards reached the last mage.

Aenor and Marius pounded down the corridor outside the hall.

"If you were a mage working for Taren, who would you target first?" gasped Aenor, sword in hand, as they raced for the common courtyard.

"The prince!"

"Right!"

"Wait!" Marius grabbed her arm and pulled her to a halt. "The final mage is a serious opponent," said Marius tersely. "He has the power of teleportation which is one of the higher aspects of battle mage training. You'd best pray that your prince is still alive."

"All vital areas in this castle are sealed with third level magic shields. Sendarion, our head battle mage, put them in place last year."

The Maester's gray eyes swung towards the prince's tower. "That will help."

Chapter 13

In the prince's tower, Marius slipped silently into antechamber leading to the prince's quarters. Standing in front of him was the missing mage, his robes gleaming softly as he tried to find a weak spot in Sanderion's spell casting. At a soft sound, he turned his head to see the Maester.

"Are they dead?" he asked casually. Marius inclined his head regally.

"You must know you're no match for me, healer."

Marius smiled like a shark. "But I've lived a lot longer than you have, and I've picked up a trick or two," he replied in a dangerously soft voice. The other mage replied with a mocking laugh.

Outside, Aenor dug her fingers and bare toes into the damp, mossy sides of the wall. She gritted her teeth impotently as she groped above her with one hand. *Now why exactly is it that I'm the one clinging to the side of a tower while he's nice and safe inside?* The wind screamed about her ears as she found another finger hold, a foot above her. Suddenly she heard a loud thud, as the window she had climbed out of slammed shut. Aenor groaned, slowly banging her forehead against the cold stone. No way back. Thankfully, the window she needed was almost beside her.

Aenor could hear the two mages trying to intimidate each other faintly through the glass. After she felt secure with her precarious position, she lifted one foot and placed it softly on the windowsill. Slowly, she shifted her weight more onto that foot, praying fervently that the old wood would hold. Searching for another finger hold that would allow her to settle into a less useless position, she couldn't help wondering what the two men inside were saying now.

"Shall we?" asked Marius with a courtly gesture. The other mage bowed politely in response, just before he emitted a stream of flame from one hand. Marius dropped to the floor in a roll, easily getting out of the way. On the way up to his feet, he whispered a quick spell. Sticky, binding threads formed around the renegade, pining his arms to his side. They dissolved an instant later, but by then Marius had his shields up and was ready for a good fight.

Aenor balanced carefully on the ledge. The wind was starting to pick up, howling like a banshee as it swept around the sides of the tower. She picked up one foot and replaced it to gain her more leverage, for when she made her grand entrance into the tower room. Her bare foot slipped off the slimy wood, throwing her off balance. Her breath froze in her chest as she scrambled for balance. Her body continued to shift backwards. No choice! She grabbed the top of the window frame with her hands and thrust herself forward towards the window.

Both mages twisted around in shock as Aenor smashed through the window with a loud yell. She felt to the floor, the broken glass crunching sickeningly under her. Marius moved instinctively, throwing himself into the body of the renegade mage. The breath left the mage's body in a loud whoosh as Marius slammed into him and knocked him to the floor. A moment later, the renegade was wrestling with the Marius, surprise and sudden anger forcing all his defensive spells from his mind. Pain exploded as a fist thudded into his face. His hands found the Marius's neck and began to squeeze for dear life.

Aenor climbed to her feet, bleeding profusely. Glass shards dug into her bare feet but she hardly felt them because she couldn't believe she wasn't a greasy spot on the cobblestones below. She stooped for her dagger before she remembered that she didn't have it anymore. Her long sword was all she had left and was much too cumbersome for use in these close quarters. In front of her, Marius and the mage were rolling around as each did their best to throttle the other. Aenor took a precious moment to enjoy the sight.

"Do something, for Mira's sake!" came a tortured croak from Marius, as he pounded the renegade's head enthusiastically against the floor.

The renegade felt cold steel slide over his throat. He could barely see because of all the stars whirling about him but he definitely felt the pressure as the flat of the blade pressed down slowly on his windpipe. Wisely deciding to cooperate, he released his hold on the Maester. That exalted personage scrambled off his victim, clutching his throat and gasping like a fish. As his vision cleared, the renegade found himself looking into a pair of very green, very deadly eyes. He felt the skin beneath the edges of the blade break and begin to trickle blood.

"In a moment, your windpipe will be crushed," came a husky voice. "Unless you tell me everything you know about this night's work."

He croaked in assent. The pressure eased just enough to enable him to talk. The mage made an immense effort to calm himself. He needed to remember his attack spells. "Taren sent me to kill the royal family. The other two were volunteered by the Abida." Aenor cast Marius a long look.

"You're lying!" hissed Marius, as he crawled over to crouch over the mage's face. "The Abida never gets involved in politics. All he's interested in is knowledge."

The renegade gave the Maester a long, measuring look. "He had something to gain this time. Your death and the guarantee that it would be done right…"

"Wonderful!" exclaimed Aenor sarcastically. "If the Abida has aligned with Lord Taren, we're in serious trouble!" She didn't see the look of concentration that entered the mage's eyes. But Marius did. Moving like a snake, he slipped his hand onto the side of the mage's neck and pinched twice. The mage's eyes faded over as he slipped down into oblivion.

Raising his head, the Maester met Aenor's questioning eyes. He shrugged in response to the unspoken query. "I don't think we would have liked what he was about to do next."

Aenor and the Maester strode into the queen's quarters. Aenor's injuries had been tended to and they were already almost completely healed. Even the nasty gash on her face looked fairly respectable. The queen was sitting in a chair talking to Tamar in a low voice, but she looked up when she heard the warriors at the door announce them.

"It seems that I owe the two of you even more thanks than before," she said with a strained smile. "Where is the Taren's pet mage now?"

"The healer is keeping him drugged in the dungeons till Sendarion returns from the Third Battalion," answered Aenor. "He'll be able to squeeze a lot more information out of the prisoner than we would."

"So. The Abida has entered the arena. That puts a whole new complexion on the matter. No one knows exactly what that one is about," said the Queen grimly. She exchanged a long look with Tamar before turning back to look directly at Aenor.

"Warrior, we have decided to act upon this new threat. The Maester has already indicated he is willing to face the Abida in a duel. What exactly would that entail?" This last question was directed towards Marius.

"He and I would face off with magic as our only weapon. The winner may claim any prize from the loser."

"But what do you intend to do to him?" pressed the Queen.

"Simply to force him to recant the vendetta he has against me," answered the Maester guardedly, as he suddenly saw the trend the conversation was taking. "I wasn't strong enough to do it before but I have learned a lot since the last time we met."

"What if we asked you to kill him on our behalf?"

"I would not do it," replied Marius firmly. "There have been times that a contestant was killed during a duel but I will not go into one with the intention of taking a life. That would be a betrayal of all that a healer believes in."

The queen nodded regretfully. "And that is the way it should be." She firmed up her resolution as she looked back up at Aenor. "Then it is up to you, warrior. It will be your duty to either kill him or force a surrender."

"Yes, Majesty. But what of my new post?" Aenor asked cautiously.

"We will hold it until your return. But you will need to bond with a new dragon so you can travel fast."

Aenor's stomach twisted in rebellion. "Majesty, Eld has barely been gone two weeks!" she protested. Tamar shot her a warning look.

"That may be, but what is a dragonrider without a dragon?" answered the queen implacably.

Tamar stepped in gracefully before Aenor could respond. "I will take care of it, my queen. However, these two have been through much and will need to rest and strategize before they head out. The Abida has lived for centuries and isn't going anywhere." The Queen smiled at that.

"You're right, Tamar. Forgive our impatience. This has been a truly trying time. Rest. We'll talk again soon."

Chapter 14

Two days later, Aenor met her aunt at the landing field. Tamar was leaning against a fence, her eyes closed and her head tilted up to catch the sun's rays. A few dragons spotted the field, drowsing in the sun.

"Ah Aenor, there you are! Ready to fly?"

"Yes Aunt, it's feels like forever since the last time," said Aenor, smiling into her aunt's kind eyes.

"Are you missing him still?"

"More each day. In truth, I really don't think I'm ready for another bonding."

"Then you must hide it, dearest. You cannot afford to offend your new bondmate. Come, two clans have young ones ready to bond. Silver Claw and Sharp Tooth. Eld was Silver Claw, wasn't he?" Aenor nodded.

"Best to visit them first then."

"I would prefer a Silver Claw," Aenor admitted. "Having one of his relatives would make it easier for me. And less of a betrayal," she added bitterly.

Tamar pulled Aenor into a tight hug. "It will pass, dearest. The day I lost Ramesh was the worst of my life but both he and Eld have gone on to better things as heroes. There are worse things than that. Come, let's go see the Silver Claws."

Tamar turned her head to face the mountains nearby and sent a telepathic call for her dragon. A few moments later, a dragon appeared flying low to skim over the fields. Aenor looked at her admiringly.

"S'aan has such beautiful form. I don't think I've seen another like her."

"Well you might soon," replied Tamar proudly. "She has her first clutch warming in the hatchery. Two more weeks, they tell me."

"Then a whole lot of hatchlings toddling after you in the barracks," laughed Aenor. "The great Tamar! Queen's Guard and dragon baby-sitter!" Tamar rolled her eyes at her.

S'aan made a smooth landing, her scales glistening in the sunlight. She was from a southern clan and showed their characteristic swirls of color. The women walked towards her. S'aan turned her massive head towards her rider.

"She says hello and that she is sorry for Eld's death," said Tamar to Aenor.

Aenor thanked S'aan for her condolences as she launched herself up behind Tamar on S'aan's bare back. A moment later, they were soaring up into the blue skies. They left the sprawling city behind them as they made for the mountains and the lair of Silver Claw Matriarch.

S'aan thumped to a halt on the jutting lip of a cave. After the warriors slid off, she spread her wings and promptly disappeared. It was wise for a lone dragon not to linger in another clan's warren.

"Kevin will meet us here shortly. Come sit by me Aenor, and tell me of your adventures."

Aenor began to summarize her journey, making her aunt chuckle at how she had taken the Maester. When she got to the part about the onset, Tamar cast her a sharp look.

"And you're telling me that he didn't even try to have sex with you?" she said in patent disbelief. Aenor shrugged her shoulders and nodded.

"All I can say is that the both of you have wills of iron! I've never been able to show such restraint during those times," Tamar said, shaking her head wryly. "Still, I'm glad you didn't lose your head. You're much too young to be saddled with children," she continued, stroking Aenor's hair affectionately. "Not that there's anything wrong with having children," she added hastily. "I so loved having you that I never felt the need to carry one myself. So what happened to your onset, anyway?"

"I don't know. After I got home, it lost strength and wound down. Perhaps the energy drain cut it short."

"Perhaps Eld's death brought on the onset early. We all deal with loss in different ways. You remember that I turned to food when I lost Ramesh?" She shuddered in remembrance. "It took me forever to shed the weight. It's possible that your body wasn't actually fertile and so it ended early. Still, you should get checked out by Astrid," lectured her aunt. "So, do you like him?" she continued archly.

"Who? The Maester? Well, I respect him and I suppose that I like him too, but I don't *like* him. He's not for me, aunt."

"Why ever not? I've looked him over. Lovely body. I wouldn't mind having a go at him myself. Those shoulders! Doesn't look like any healer I've ever seen!"

Aenor colored. Her aunt was renowned for letting the world know when she admired a man. Suddenly she had a vision of her slender aunt tackling the unwary Maester and having her wicked way with him. *Tearing off his shirt, pulling off his breaches...* Aenor blinked rapidly, disconcerted. Tamar was wearing a very self-satisfied look on her face.

"So you're not as immune to him as you're trying to get me to think." She ignored her niece's glare and continued smugly. "Give it up, girl. I see all! And let me pass on a valuable piece of wisdom. Men are wonderful.

You should enjoy them for all you're worth and when you're done, give them an unforgettable kiss and walk away." Aenor snorted inelegantly.

"Right. So that's why you've been with Maten for the last two years."

"Well the man just grew on me. Somewhat like a fungus," replied Tamar regretfully. "Things like that happen sometimes. Everybody's philandering days come to an end with a single look and a wrench of the heart. But until that unhappy day, young one, enjoy life to fullest! You have a lifetime ahead of you, Aenor. Don't rush into love any time soon, all right?"

"Tamar. Aenor. Sorry I'm late," puffed a tall, gray haired man as he climbed up the steep path from the rocky valley below. "Treven is expecting us, so let's hurry to her." The two women followed him into the dank cave, moving deeper and deeper into it until only the light of Kevin's lantern showed their way. The walls were damp and dripping constantly and there was definitely a smell of wet dragon in the air.

"She likes it in here because of her scales, you know. She's had such a problem with them as she aged, poor thing. The moisture helps quite a bit."

Suddenly they emerged from the wide tunnel into a large cavern deep in the mountain's belly. And curled up in the center of the cavern was the largest dragon in the clan. As the group approached her, Treven the matriarch of the Silver Claw clan, uncoiled her white body to greet them. She was so large that her hindquarters disappeared into the darkness beyond the lantern light. Blazing reptilian eyes, undimmed by age, regarded them with interest.

"Treven. This is Tamar and you remember Aenor," introduced Kevin to his partner.

Aenor gasped as a faint but resonant voice sounded in her head. Yes, I remember you. The golden eyes looked at her with amusement.

Are you surprised at hearing me? Doesn't my son's essence flow in your veins?

It was you! You sent the dragons to escort us in!

Yes. Your call was faint but it had undertones of my son's voice. That's when I knew for sure that Eld had left this world. I could not refuse your plea for aid.

"Thank you for your help, Matriarch," answered Aenor aloud. "I want you to know that Eld died well." The massive head lifted, the foot long horns on her frill grazing the ceiling of the cavern.

Yes, he did. I am very proud of him. I expect I shall be seeing him soon.

"Nonsense, Treven," scoffed Kevin. "You'll outlive us all!"

"I would like to petition you for another bondmate, Matriarch. I will be going on a critical mission shortly and I'll need the help," said Aenor.

The massive head dipped in consideration.

The Dragonrider's Quest

Eld always spoke of you with great fondness. He would want me to grant your wish. I like you as well, Aenor. Your heart is steady and there is no guile in you. It is my hope that one of my hatchlings chooses you for his or her own. Come out into the air with me.

Once they were back at the mouth of the cave, the matriarch sent out a loud, booming call. In minutes, three young dragons circled outside the warren and landed, one at a time, on the cave ledge. Aenor stepped forward to face them.

This is Aenor of the Prince's Guard. She is putting herself forward as a bondmate. Do any of you want her?

Three large snouts dipped to sniff at Aenor. Her scent would tell them much of her character and of their compatibility. Swiftly the midnight blue female on the right put a leg forward to claim her.

Lya. You wish her? Aenor couldn't hear the female's response but it must have been positive because the matriarch turned to her.

Aenor, this is my daughter from my second last clutch. Her name is Lya and she has consented to bind with you. Will you accept her?

Aenor turned to look at the young female. Bright intelligent eyes regarded her in return. Although she didn't have a telepathic bond with her yet, she sensed that the dragon would be as close a friend as Eld ever was. *His sister! What a wonderful thing!*

"It would be my honor."

Tamar and Kevin broke out into congratulatory handshakes.

"The binding should be held tonight so the three of you can set out in a few days. Once you are recovered, that is," said Tamar. Kevin translated for all the dragons. Lya dipped her massive head in acknowledgment.

"Lya said that she will be at the main barracks, at the seventh hour."

Aenor felt her stomach clench involuntarily. The last binding had been agonizing for her. She had barely lived. Perhaps the second would be easier.

Chapter 15

Aenor concentrated on controlling her breathing as she went into the final set of exercises. Her long sword whirled about her in graceful patterns as she focused on an imaginary foe. Practicing always kept her mind from its worries. The smooth steel flashed in the fading light as she came back into the ready stance. Once she was done, she turned her head towards the west, shading her eyes as she sought out the grand water clock that loomed over the palace compound.

"Gods!" she exclaimed as she took off towards her quarters at a run. Twenty minutes later, she was wrestling with her wet hair when a knock sounded at her door.

"Ready? Oh, I guess not," said Tamar wryly as she plopped down on Aenor's bed. "Need some help?"

"No, I've got everything under control," mumbled Aenor as she tugged large amounts of hair from the brush. Leaving her hair to dry on its own, she pulled out a brand new uniform in the prince's colors.

"Mira! Why does Zara always think that I starve myself!" she swore in an undertone as she struggled into the form-fitting navy uniform. Her ceremonial armor went on next and finally the heavy navy cape that clipped onto her shoulders. She gave herself a once over in the mirror, cape swirling dramatically around her. She signed. Flashy and totally impractical. In some deep, dark part of her, the last vestiges of her vanity were grateful that all that navy didn't clash with her hair.

The two women arrived at the barracks just a few minutes before the seventh hour. Aenor grimaced as she saw the glass apparatus laid out on a table in the square. One of the dragon handlers fished a sharp dagger from a pot of boiling water and laid it down beside the other implements. He turned at the sound of their approach.

"Well now. Here's half of the pair," he said cheerfully. "And what do you know! Here comes the other half." He gestured towards the sky.

Lya swept in for a landing, her mother following close behind her, decked out in her best. Her freshly polished scales gleamed a deep blue as the shifting patterns of the firelight flowed over her sturdy body. Silver trappings sparkled madly on her forehead and flanked as she shifted over to make room for her parent. Treven, with Kevin on her back, landed and folded up her wings efficiently. The matriarch acknowledged everyone in the square with a regal nod. Then the handler gestured Aenor towards Lya.

"These two have chosen to be bonded. Is there anything I should know before we perform the binding? No? Good. Then let us start."

The handler picked up a glass bottle, connected a short length of hose to it and, finally, a wickedly sharp glass tube to the free end. He walked over to Lya, located a vein at her elbow and jabbed through her thick hide with the skewer. Thick, black ichor oozed into the bottle. When the bottle had filled, the handler withdrew the skewer and an assistant swabbed the cut, opting to let it heal naturally.

The handler positioned the bottle on top of a small flame and connected it up to the series of glass vessels. Over the next few minutes, the ichor boiled, releasing a vapor that condensed into a faintly green fluid. When he had a small amount collected, he cooled the vial in some water and drew it up into a large syringe.

"Are you ready?" he asked one last time. Aenor nodded, the line of her jaw firming as she held forth her arm. "Don't worry, it won't be that bad."

The essence hit her system in a wave of heat. Aenor felt her stomach heave sickeningly, as her body struggled to repel the foreign substance. She bent over gasping, curling up in an instinctual move to lessen the pain. Then suddenly, her sight blurred as her legs weakened and she slowly folded to her knees. She barely felt the touch of Tamar's hands on her shoulders, keeping her vertical. Disjointed voices faded in and out of her mind, flashes of images she had never seen.

116

Then a strangely comforting voice cutting through the chaos. *I'm here, Aenor. Lean on me.*

Lya, she thought gratefully, as the empty corner in her mind that was Eld's, filled with a new presence.

Tamar and Kevin bent over Aenor's kneeling body, checking her vital signs. Her forehead burned unnaturally hot. "She's having another bad reaction," said Tamar grimly. "Get Astrid! Now!"

Astrid swept into Aenor's quarters with the Maester on her heels. Aenor had been undressed and wrapped in damp cloths, with chunks of ice scattered over her. Marius held back gracefully, to indicate that Astrid had jurisdiction here. A swift examination and Astrid stood up to discuss the situation with the Maester and a grim Tamar.

"Her heart rate is too high. The heart muscles won't be able to take it for long. We need to slow it down before her heart itself bursts. What do you think, my lord? Ice to bring her temperature down and foxroot to slow her heart rate?"

"Yes, I think that's all we can do. Aenor is physically very tough. Once her body's functions are back within a normal range, she should recover fairly quickly."

"Wait, my lords," broke in Tamar tensely. "There is something you should know. There could be a complication. The last time this happened, Aenor told me

117

that… she met her mother in the realm she was in. You see, her parents died twenty years ago, quite horribly. The neighbors managed to keep Aenor from running into the house to see, but she must have overheard them talking. Right after that night, she started having nightmares of poor Kira's death."

"How did they die?" asked the Maester.

"Kira was a journeyman mage. She had discovered a grimoire in her Maester's library, dealing with the calling of demons…" The healers cast grim looks at each other, quickly figuring out what had happened. "She wasn't strong enough to control the creature. It ripped her into little pieces. My brother died when he broke into her workroom to help her." Astrid glanced over at her former teacher.

"That could explain why she's having such a bad reaction. If she inherited latent magical abilities, a binding could have opened up unused pathways in her brain."

"Aenor refused to be tested for battle mage training so I don't know if she does have any such abilities." Tamar sat down on the bed and took Aenor's burning hand in her own. "The last time Aenor went under, she met a demon who had taken her mother's form. She said it tried to kill her. There was a lot more to it I'm sure, because Aenor refused to ever discuss it with me again. I'm afraid that's what's happening now. She said that she barely got away the last time. I don't know if she can do it again…"

"Aenor my dear, you're back," purred a beloved voice in her ear. Aenor closed her eyes slowly before drawing her sword and turning to face a very familiar figure.

"Go back to the abyss, demon spawn, before I chop you into little pieces."

The auburn-haired woman with the glowing eyes laughed delightedly. "Oh my dear, entertaining as ever! As if you could defeat me... All you have is that pathetic sword. I have all the endless power of the universe to use."

"Is that why I got away the last time?" goaded Aenor. "You're nothing but a third rate imp with delusions of grandeur. You're pathetic."

Demon-Kira's eyes flamed as its voice dropped menacingly. "Could a third rate imp have done this to that tasty little morsel you called a mother?" Suddenly, the figure standing in front of Aenor truly was her mother. The eyes were terrified and completely human. Kira backed away from Aenor in horror.

"Aenor, RUN!"

"Mama!" gasped Aenor.

"Run!" screamed the woman, as she suddenly convulsed in agony as a dripping black tentacle forced its way out of one eyeball. Her body started to rip apart to reveal something hideous and black within it, even as the screams continued. Aenor froze up. She squeezed her eyes shut, as her worst childhood nightmares became reality.

The Maester and Tamar were holding a shrieking Aenor down onto the bed. From outside, came a dragon scream as Lya felt her partner's unreasoning terror through the barely established bond.

The Dragonrider's Quest

"The dragon!" said Marius, looking over at Tamar in sudden hope. "We can reach her through the dragon!"

He leapt out the ground floor window, heading towards Lya at a run. She was lying on the ground, twitching as her mother and another dragon splattered mud onto her body with their wings to bring her temperature down. Kevin ran to meet Marius.

"Lya says that she doesn't know how to help Aenor. The bond is too undeveloped and the pain has crippled her mind."

"Tell her that we can still use the bond to help Aenor. If she agrees to let me in her mind, I can find Aenor." Kevin translated to Treven who in turn telepathed the message to Lya. The younger dragon's eyes flashed and rolled as she whimpered in terror and agony.

"She agrees! Do whatever you have to."

The Maester drove into the dragon's mind and gasped. So much pain! Beside him was the shadowy form of the dragon's being. He reached out to channel some of his strength to it and the pain instantly eased. *Now,* he telepathed, *follow the screaming!* The dragon spread her shadowy wings and shot off into the void with the Maester, in falcon form, close behind. They cut through the shifting colors, using the sound of Aenor's shrieks as their guide. But then, the screams suddenly cut off. Thankfully, they had come far enough. The pair slammed through a black wall into Aenor's world.

In front of them, Aenor lay unconscious with blue fire flickering over her body and surrounded by gore. Both her arms had been torn off her body, one still clutching her sword. A black, hulking monstrosity crouched chuckling over the remnants of her body as it prepared to rip her legs off. Fury rose within Marius, burning bright, filling him with inhuman energy. His existence coalesced into a single, grinding thought. Destroy! He felt himself morph into his human form as he willed an image of a broadsword into his hands. The dragon life-force beside him suddenly expanded in size as it screamed a blazingly furious challenge. A distinct shape began to emerge, that of Lya in her full physical glory.

The creature looked up at Marius and grinned evilly. It took hold of one of Aenor's legs and prepared to twist it off. The broadsword swung and took off the creature's head. The head bounced away a short distance and began to chuckle as the creature's body continued with its work. Aenor's leg snapped like a twig in its hands. Then a gale force wind descended with the sound of flapping wings and knocked Marius to the ground. Spirit-Lya yanked the creature away from Aenor and soared up and away with it dangling from her claws. As she began to dismember the creature in her rage, Marius walked over to the creature's grinning head and stamped it into a pulp with his heel.

The red curtain of rage faded into fear as Marius took Aenor's destroyed inner-self into his arms. Above him, Spirit-Lya continued to shriek in fury as she tore the demon apart. Marius's heart skipped a beat as he bowed his head and began to beg Mira silently to keep Aenor unconscious. If she awoke, thinking herself dismembered, the shock would make the healing all the harder. He began to draw on his reserves, building and concentrating his power for the next stage: erasing this whole thing from her memory. He pushed into her mind, using Lya as his link and searched for her last memory. When he found it, it began to play for him, showing him all that she had endured. He didn't wait to see it all. He took hold of it and ripped it forcibly out of her.

As Spirit-Lya landed beside them to nose gently at her bondmate, Marius looked up into her intelligent eyes. He never let go of Aenor as Lya flew them both back into reality.

Chapter 16

Aenor opened her eyes to see the light of a new day. She blinked rapidly, shading her eyes with one hand as she groaned and turned away from the glare. As she did, her gaze felt upon the sleeping pair sitting in the uncomfortable chairs beside her. As she lifted her head from the pillow to stare at them in puzzlement, a golden voice spoke in her mind.

Are you all right?

Aenor gasped in disbelief. *Eld?*

There was a slight pause. *No, this is Lya. Do you remember the bonding?*

Aenor blinked in confusion as she struggled to regain her equilibrium. She remembered the meeting with the matriarch clearly but everything after that seemed incomplete. Flashes of memory that she vainly tried to reach but couldn't recover. Then suddenly she felt the touch of another mind, a questing dragon mind. As soon as it came, it withdrew from her.

It matters not. You're well now and we're safely paired, came the voice reassuringly. Aenor sank back into the comfort of her bed, pulling the covers up to chest level, suddenly feeling that everybody knew something she didn't.

Something happened, I know it. I can feel it in my soul. Tell me.

You had a bad reaction to the binding. Aenor became very still. Suddenly the warm morning light seemed to be touched with a tinge of coldness. Something crystallized in a corner of her mind but even as she strained towards it, it melted away.

You have been unconscious for two days now and we were all worried that you would die from it. The healers have been with you continuously, feeding you all sorts of potions and spells. Their care has obviously been rewarded. Here you are, none the worst for the experience, finished Lya blithely.

Aenor accepted the explanation grudgingly. It was hard to be suspicious with sunlight dancing in the corners of the room and the pleasure of having a partner to talk with again. She swung her feet to the floor and made a vain clutch for the covers as she suddenly realized that she was nude under the sheets. Her eyes came to rest on the sleeping figures of her aunt and Marius scrunched up like accordions in the stiff, wicker chairs. She put out a hand to rouse them, but something made her draw it back. A vision of the Maester holding an old-fashioned broadsword, feet braced apart, with fire in his eyes. As soon as the picture came, it was gone, leaving her puzzled and wondering vainly what a healer would be doing with a sword in his hands. She shrugged the thought off and settled back instead, to regard him quietly.

In sleep, his face was relaxed, yet it retained the character that he had acquired through his many centuries. If he were a normal man, he would definitely draw a second look from her. And perhaps a third. Her aunt's words came back to whisper in her mind: *Lovely body!*

She had to admit that her aunt was right. Physically, he was very nice. Thick, wavy hair, wonderfully broad shoulders, trim waist, long muscled legs, strong thick penis. As she remembered him standing by that well, pouring water over his long, lithe body, she felt the delicious thrill of attraction flare up again. *Now that we are fated to travel together on yet another quest, isn't foolish to continue denying it?*

No, replied Aenor's brain firmly. This is strictly business. *I need to be focused right now. But, wouldn't it be oh, so satisfying,* whispered her body. Aenor shoved the renegade thought aside as she shook the sleeping pair awake. First things first. She had a dragon to get acquainted with.

Five days later, Aenor and Marius were summoned to the queen's quarters. As they entered, they found Selene talking to a tall, stately man dressed in red and black robes. Sendarion, the battle mage.

"The renegade had revealed the location of the Abida's fortress," said the queen to the pair abruptly. "It lies in the furthest sanction of this land, up in the north."

Great, thought Aenor to herself. *Now I'm going to be frozen to death...* Marius thanked the queen and the battle mage courteously, never mentioning that he had always known where the Abida was. They could sense each other.

"When can you leave?"

Aenor exchanged a glance with the Maester, reaching a consensus instantly. "The sooner the better, Majesty. We just need to get set up for the journey."

"You do know that you can't be associated with this court, don't you warrior?" stated the queen sternly. "Thanks to the Maester's announcement of his intentions in full court, everybody thinks that you are a bodyguard, nothing more. And that's the way it has to stay." Marius inclined his head in acknowledgment.

"Then I obviously can't go in the uniform of a prince's guard," murmured Aenor, half to herself. "In fact, we should both look as normal as possible... The northern sanctions are Taren's territory. No one will look twice at a pair of mercenaries traveling to join his army."

"The Abida will see us coming, but at least we won't have to deal with trouble from the local populace," replied Marius. "It might make sense for us to leave in secret, just in case Taren has spies somewhere in the castle." The queen cracked a grim smile at that.

"My lord, I can guarantee that Taren has spies in this castle and that they have been watching you with a great deal of interest. You're a living legend and there is power in that. You could be prove very useful in a power struggle." The Maester's eyes suddenly turned cold.

"Majesty, I want you to understand that I am not going to be drawn into a political situation. I am not of your country and Huria stands neutral in your conflict," he stated in a low and firm voice. "I will not interfere with Aenor's mission as long as she doesn't interfere with mine. That means that I will get the first shot at the Abida. Whatever the warrior does, she does after the duel!" This drew an angry look from Aenor. "That part of the mission is wholly and completely separate from mine."

The queen's face stiffened. "I understand, my lord. I can hardly dictate terms as I owe you my son's life."

"But I must protest, Your Majesty!" Aenor broke in. "I am being sent as an assassin! I can't be restrained by all these rules. I must take any chance I find to terminate the target."

"Not if you travel with me, Aenor," replied Marius smoothly.

"The thing is, Marius, you need me more than I need you," answered Aenor equally firmly, as she turned to look him straight in the eye. "I can travel on my own and get the job done just as well."

"I think not, warrior. The Abida's citadel is protected not only by human guards but also by his elemental creations and a series of intricate spells. Without me, you wouldn't get past the first level."

"And without me, you wouldn't live to get there!"

"Just how do you imagine that I've survived the last 400 years without you?"

Sendarion seemed fascinated by tug of words, the chaotic mix of first names and titles. He was a man that looked for weaknesses and he had already found both of theirs.

"It seems that the two of you need to reach a compromise," interrupted the queen, losing patience with the wordplay. "I agree with Aenor in that she should take advantage of any opportunity to complete her mission but I also agree with you in that she should not interfere with your task or that you become involved in our political games. If the two of you feel that you cannot work together on this, speak up now and we'll find someone else to do the job!"

Aenor and Marius didn't look at each other as they considered the queen's ultimatum. "The Maester and I will continue to discuss this after we leave Miramar," said Aenor stiffly, as she broke the uncomfortable impasse. Marius didn't contradict her, so she continued. "We will sneak out of the palace compound as soon as our disguises are ready."

"We'll need to get you armed," said Aenor to Marius as they left the queen's chambers. "I don't know much about healer training, what weapons are you trained to handle?"

"The training doesn't include anything on weaponry, but I was trained in the use of the broadsword, axe and staff in my youth." Aenor grimaced. All those were heavy and cumbersome weapons. "I stopped weapons use when I became a healer, so I'm definitely more comfortable with my magic than with my weapon skills," he continued frankly.

"Oh well, we'll get in some practice time during our journey," sighed Aenor. "I've been a little lax myself these past few weeks."

"Just a staff, I think. I should make *some* attempt at living up to a healer's values."

"Marius, the north is in chaos. You'd stick out like a sore thumb if you're *not* bristling with weaponry."

"Well, that's what you're for," Marius with a grin, whacking her shoulder in a comradely manner. "You'll have to do the intimating for the both of us. I'll take care of the bandaging..."

"Great. We're doomed."

That night, two figures dressed in mercenary leathers sneaked out of the northern gates of the palace compound. As they disappeared into the darkness, a large dark shape swept silently over the palace walls and soared up into the black velvet sky.

Chapter 17

The old man looked up from his whittling to check out the newest arrivals in Vela. He snorted derisively. More mercenaries. His town seemed to have become their favorite stop. This pair was unusual though. They came in on foot. Obviously they had fallen on hard times. Either that or they were no good. They sauntered past him like they knew what they were doing though. The woman had her hand resting casually on her hilt while the man had the look of power in his eyes. The old man hadn't been a slave trader for 30 years without knowing how to read people and he quickly dismissed the pair as capable killers. He turned back to his carving without another look.

Dust swirled around booted feet as the pair ducked into a trainer's shop. When they emerged a half hour later, the old man looked up to see the trainer hand the reins of two large tuktus to them. He processed the information quickly. Obviously heading north if they were buying winter mounts. He watched them swing onto the shaggy backs of the snorting beasts and adjust their fur cloaks to cover them from shoulder to knee. *Good, they're not staying.* He wondered idly if they would survive the northern blizzards, then promptly forgot them as the pair thundered past him heading north.

The tuktus skittered nervously as soon as they smelt dragon in the air. A moment later, a blue dragon thudded to a halt in front of them. Both Aenor and the Maester had to pull in the reins to hold the nervous beasts steady as Lya folded in her wings neatly. She had saved them a phenomenal amount of travel time but this was where she would stay while they continued onwards. The colder climes of the north played havoc with reptilian biology. The last thing they needed was a sick or hibernating dragon on their hands.

Do you have everything you need? Lya asked, as the pair dismounted and lashed the tuktus to a nearby branch. The shaggy beasts instantly pulled away to the other side of the tree for safety.

Yes, I think so. Food and clothing. And weapons. Can you think of anything else?

What about spell books for the mage?

He has them. We checked them out from the mage-school at Miramar. Anything else?

I think that's it. Are those things vegetarian? Lya gestured to the huddled tuktus with her snout.

Yes, but I don't think that will be a problem. They eat foliage of any kind.

131

Then you're set. I'll fly up to the caverns in those hills over there. Now remember, call if you need me. I'll hear you wherever you are…

Aenor nodded and patted the dragon's side with a smile. *I will, Lya.*

The dragon crouched low and then took off in a gust of wind. The Maester shielded his eyes from the dust as he watched her go.

"Ready?" came Aenor's voice from behind him. He turned to face her and nodded.

Later that evening, they dismounted with groans at their chosen campsite. In unspoken agreement, they dumped their bedrolls to the ground and collapsed on top of them. To people accustomed to the smooth glide of a dragon, the rough jolting gait of a tuktu could cause aches and pains in muscles that had never announced their presence before. As Marius lay motionless upon the ground, staring up at the sky, he suddenly spoke in a drained voice.

"I'll flip you for who gets to make supper…"

Aenor groaned softly in reply. "I can't even move to get the coin…" They lay silent a while longer. Then Marius spoke up again.

"If I produce the coin, will you flip for dinner?"

"Only if you'll lose…" Silence reigned once more.

"How about we forget about dinner?"

"Sounds good to me." They both rolled over in their blankets and fell asleep.

The next day, amidst yelps of pain, the pair continued north. A definite chill entered the air as the vegetation around them started to take on the look of the cold lands. Spring had definitely not made it this far yet. Huddling within her furs, Aenor could only be grateful that leather was a decent insulator. She glanced over at Marius, who rose beside her, gracefully balancing a spell book on the pommel of the saddle. His lips moved silently, one hand occasionally tracing arcane symbols in the air. Bored already, Aenor turned back to the landscape as their mounts plodded on gamely.

That night, they camped by a mountain stream. After roasting a couple of plump pigeons Aenor had shot from the sky, they each took a bath with lukewarm water and settled by the fire to rest. Marius glanced over at Aenor who was sitting across from him, staring meditatively into the fire.

"I never congratulated you on your promotion," he said. "Although, to be frank, I don't know if it's a promotion or a lateral move."

"Oh, it's definitely a move in the right direction," she replied with feeling. "I was hoping for something like this, so it definitely feels good.

"When I first entered military life, I had an affair with the prince," she continued frankly. Marius kept silent, although he was set off-balance by both her admission and the fact that she was actually opening up. "That got me transferred to the Dragonrider Corps. It wasn't too bad. I trained with this cranky old warrior. He taught me that a dragon and a good sword are the most valuable allies a warrior can have. I can still hear him say: 'Always be good to both of them. One can fail you, the other can eat you.' He was a bit of a windbag but in a tight spot, there was no one else I would rather have at my back. When the war started, Eld and I went to the front. We saw a good bit of action, usually got out by the skin of our teeth and lost some friends. We were rotated back to the capital a few months ago and we just happened to be the closest pair when the prince was attacked. Just lucky, I guess," she added with a half-smile.

"So now you're in the Prince's Guard. Isn't that going to be a tad awkward for the two of you?"

Aenor made a face. "Probably. I was hoping for the Queen's Guard but it would have looked like favoritism if both my aunt and I are in the same squad. Plus the Prince's Guard was decimated as part of the attack. It makes sense to stick me there." Aenor leaned forward to wrap her arms around her knees. "I don't have feelings for the prince, if you're wondering. It was a long, long time ago and I was a different person."

"My turn," Aenor flipped the questioning. "So. The Abida. You killed his mother, right?"

134

Marius's eyebrows shot skyward. "Tactfully done, there."

"Well, it would be helpful if I had the background."

Marius shook his head. "It's not a pretty story and I can't share all the details"

"I'll take anything that I can get."

"Where do I even start? Margary was a truly extraordinary mage. She had made the study of the art her life's work and was operating leaps and bounds beyond her peers. Truly cutting edge. I believe that she was the first Ageless but I never found out how she turned. By the time I met her, she and her son Ryce were living in an ancient castle called Bodian deep in the northern mountains."

"As for me, I was the son of a merchant but born with talent. As I told you, my first inclination was to study to be a battle mage. I was about to complete my studies in Huria when rumors reached me that Margary was looking to take on a new apprentice. To make a long story short, I was very motivated to learn from her and so spent a year trying to find her location. Eventually, the combination of rumors and conjecture led me to her, deep in the northern mountains. I was one of two that made it there. Myself and a Norwellian named Huell."

"We were the only young men there. Ryce was a few years older than me but he was not yet Ageless. A decent fellow, but birth complications had left him with a malformed pelvic girdle that caused him to limp. I found out eventually that the reason that Margary had not changed him was because she wanted a better body for him to spend eternity in."

Aenor paled, understanding where the tale was going. Marius nodded at her. "You've already guessed. Huell and I were prospective replacements for Ryce's body. I don't think Ryce knew what his mother was about, as he invested hours of his time instructing us on battle magic, mind control as well as potions and spell craft."

"About six months after we arrived, Margary drugged Huell and I and moved us down into her workshop deep in the heart of the mountain. She had come up with a procedure of transferring a consciousness between bodies and she needed test subjects. When I awoke, I had been forced out of my body and was lost in the Darklands. I searched for a way back for days it seemed. It was only by luck that I found my own trail and followed it back to my body. When I slipped back in and awoke, I found myself tied down and Margary was in the process of making my body Ageless," he said bitterly. "The funny thing is that people assume that I killed her to get the secret to eternal life but the reality is that I have no idea how she did it. Ryce obviously did, because he turned himself."

"Anyway, while Margary continued to work on me, Huell awakened and began working free of his restraints. He got free and dragged her away from me. Unfortunately, he was no match for her. She grabbed his face and started draining him. In my terror, my new powers flared out of control and I accidently set fire to my clothes and bonds." Marius rubbed his leg unconsciously as if remembering the pain. "When my bonds finally burned off, I grabbed a dagger from a table nearby and stabbed Margary in the back. It was too late for Huell though. He was already dead."

"So there you have it. That's what really happened." Marius leant back, giving her a level look. "I have absolutely no regrets for killing Margary. But Ryce couldn't forgive, even after he came down to the workshop and saw the carnage with his own eyes. He could easily have ended me then with no one the wiser. But as I said, he was a decent man. Once he figured out that it was his mother that had betrayed the bond between teacher and student, he let me live. He healed me before turning me out, warning me to get out of Norwall and never come back. I was only too happy to oblige. Ryce went on to become known as the Abida."

Aenor was silent for a moment, absorbing the tale. Then she said, "I can't reconcile your description of Ryce with what we know of the Abida."

"He is powerful and reclusive, yes. But have you heard of him harming anyone without cause? He rightfully destroys anyone who comes looking to become Ageless as he clearly understands its potential for misuse. Could you imagine the queen and Taren both being Ageless? It would be never-ending strife. In my book, he has been a most responsible keeper of the secret."

The passion with which Marius defended his supposed enemy both surprised and warmed Aenor. Deep inside, the last remnant of her distrust collapsed. "Do you regret being Ageless?"

"Yes and no. True, it has set me apart but it has also allowed me to experience so much more than most people get the chance to do. I've travelled and seen the world. I've loved and lost. I've fought and I've taught. I've killed and I've healed. I just wish that it had been my choice rather than being forced on me."

"If you were offered the choice today, would you choose to be Ageless?"

"Probably," he replied. "I've a lot more to learn and teach. I don't think I've wasted my time, except for a few years here and there." She smiled at that.

"Well, at least you're honest about it," she said, as she arranged her bedroll beside the fire. "Let's get to sleep. The sooner we find the Abida, the sooner we can get back to the south."

Chapter 18

The next morning, snow flurries began to swirl around them as they continued onwards. The sky took on a leaden, gray shade. In the distance were the mountains they were heading for, their majestic peaks lost in the cloud cover. By mid-afternoon, they had reached the range's foothills. Nestled in an evergreen valley was a small mountain station, a stop on the fur trading route. The roads were ill made but the buildings were durable. The companions drew their mounts to a halt in front of what looked to be an inn. Aenor sent a hungry look at the sign in the window that proclaimed that the establishment had 'the best food in this sanction'. At this point, she didn't really care what it tasted like as long as it was hot.

They were settled at a table with mugs of brown ale, awaiting their feast. The inn was a rough sort of place, its patrons looking like they had scorned baths their whole life. Aenor could feel the surly glances from the other patrons and the hairs on the back of her neck prickled. Still, her hand was steady as she lifted her mug to her lips. Across from her, the Maester laid his staff visibly across the table and studiously ignored his surroundings. One finger tapped a quick rhythm on the table as he waited for nourishment. Then suddenly, a voice came from behind Aenor.

"You looking for work?" Aenor turned slowly around in her chair.

"Not at the moment. We're traveling to join Lord Taren's army," Marius answered. The large, burly man grunted in reply, his eyes suddenly dropping to look interestedly at Aenor's form.

"What about you, sweetheart?" he leered at her.

"You heard my companion," she replied evenly. "We're going to fight for Taren." A bellow of laughter replied which spread to the other occupants of the inn.

"The little chicklet thinks she can fight in Taren's army!" He turned back to face Aenor, who rose to her feet with a dangerous glint in her eye. "What makes you think you're good enough to survive a war?"

"Do you really want to find out?" she answered lazily, her eyes dangerously bland as she regarded the mountain of a man in front of her. The man paused at that.

"Look, we're not here to make trouble," broke in Marius evenly. "We're just hungry and tired mercs. Pick a fight with us and you'll get a lot more than you bargained for." The man-mountain puffed up like an angry rooster at the implication. A rough hand descended on Aenor's shoulder. Aenor went silently into action. Her foot shot out and hooked around the man's ankle. A moment later, she had the point of her sword at his throat, as he lay flat on the floor.

"Anybody else want to play?" she asked the room with a cold smile on her lips. All eyes returned studiously to their former positions. The man at her feet growled. Aenor pressed the tip of her sword deeper into his flesh to encourage him to shut up. He did so instantly.

"Now, you can leave this place two ways," she said, looking down. "Intact or in several pieces. Take your pick!" A moment later, Aenor sat back down and met the Maester's amused gaze. She shrugged casually and tore in a piece of dry bread with her teeth.

After finishing their meal, the companions gathered up their belongings and headed out the door. Fur swirled around their booted feet as they stepped back out into the cold. As Aenor exited, someone grabbed her shoulder and swung her around to slam her into the outer wall of the building. She gasped in pain and began to see stars. Beside her, she heard the hiss of skin against wood as the Maester drew his staff. Suddenly, she felt cold metal at her throat as her assailant held a dagger to her skin. Her sight cleared to see Marius facing off with a swordsman. Her captor was the man from inside the inn. Liquor tainted breath flooded into her face as the man took a better hold of her, crudely grabbing her breast. Fury colored her vision for a few seconds but she dared not move until she felt that he was distracted enough. Meanwhile, Marius and his opponent had started circling each other, weapons at the ready.

Marius struck first. Moving like a snake, he swung at his opponent's legs. The man leapt into the air, narrowly missing the blade and retaliated with a swipe at the Maester's midsection. Marius saw the move coming so he hunched his back to get his stomach out of the way. The tip of the blade sliced through his leather shirt and grazed his flesh, leaving a thin red line. He then swung his foot in the manner he had seen Aenor use and successfully threw his opponent off balance. As the man stumbled against a wall, Marius sprang after him. Aenor heard her captor hiss and took advantage of his distraction by ramming her elbow up backwards into his midsection. The dagger at her throat sliced slightly into her throat, but fell away as the man doubled up in pain.

Aenor stepped away from him and turned slowly to face him. She grabbed his shirt with her left hand, propping him up as she began to soothe her wounded pride by working him over with her right. As a grand finale, she drove her knee into his groin, before allowing him to slide slowly down to the floor. As she turned, feeling fairly satisfied, she saw the Maester drive the end of his staff into his opponent's stomach and then spin it to whack him in the side of the head. The man crumpled slowly to the ground and let out a slow groan as he slid into unconsciousness.

"Ready to go?" Marius asked politely, as he turned away from the prone figure. Aenor threw him a grin and nodded.

The rest of the day, they rode companionably together as their mounts picked their way carefully up a crude mountain path. Around them, loomed giant evergreens, their foliage masking the sight of the sky from the pair below. Aenor shivered as she drew her gray wolf cloak tighter about her body. The temperature seemed to have dropped a further ten degrees in the shady green depths of the woods. Good cover but still uncomfortable to a woman born and bred in the warm, dry regions of the central sanctions. The silence around them was beautiful. No bird song crossed the air but none was needed. It almost felt like a holy place, gentle and unassuming. Then the Maester broke the silence.

"You still haven't assured me that I will have first shot at the Abida."

"You're right," she answered with a bland smile.

"This has been my fight much, much longer than yours."

"Yes, but I've sworn to protect the queen's interests in this matter and, quite frankly, she pays my wages, not you."

"Aenor," the Maester spoke quietly, his eyes fixed in the distance. "Don't fight me on this. You're out of your league with him." Aenor turned her head slowly to look at him, one eyebrow arched in an elegantly disbelieving look.

"Don't put all your coin on it." She dug her knees into her tuktu's sides, urging it into a faster trot.

Chapter 19

Darkness fell with astonishing speed. Suddenly, the pair found themselves foundering around in the dark with no camp prepared and no food cooking. The cold was flesh numbing. Aenor swore imaginatively under her breath. Finding firewood in the dark wasn't her favorite thing to do when she was cold and hungry. Nevertheless, between the two of them, they gathered enough brush to build a decent fire. After a dinner of warmed jerky, the two of them sat huddled against the rustling wind that had suddenly sprung up, alternately warming and rubbing their gloved hands together. Aenor produced a flash of *viaska* and gasped as the fiery liquid burned its way down her throat. As she handed it over to Marius, the alcohol burn spread throughout her body and down into her numbed toes.

"Gods! This is wonderful," gasped Marius, as he choked back a slug of the potent liquid. "Enough of this stuff and I won't need these stinky furs."

"Enough of that stuff, and you'll be a dead man!" joked Aenor, as she wrapped herself up most securely in her furs, pulled up her hood and lay down as close to the fire as she dared. "We're going to need a lot more of that stuff where we're going."

She lifted her head to look over at the man opposite her with a suddenly serious look in her eyes. "You should sleep with me tonight for warmth. I've heard of people going to sleep in these mountains never to wake up."

Marius shot her a quick glance, nodded briskly and stood up, looking very much like a bear in his voluminous layers.

Aenor heard the thud of his bedroll behind her and the rustle of the furs as he unfolded it. Next a gloriously warm body descended to nestle up against her back.

"Here," came a hand over her side. "We should use both our cloaks as blankets and tuck them in as close to our bodies as possible."

Aenor handed him the edge of her cloak and the two of them wriggled around within the cocoon of their wrappings, until their bodies were lying skin to skin surrounded by a nest of furs. Aenor turned her body to face the fire, away from him. A moment later, she felt his body fit itself to the contours of hers, one arm hesitantly coming over her body to curl about her waist. Aenor sighed as a blissful warmth invaded her body, his warm breath flowing over the back of her neck like a soothing caress as their leathers clung together, glued by their natural oils. All in all, a very pleasant state of affairs. They snuggled closer instinctively.

145

The Dragonrider's Quest

Time passed. The Maester lay awake in the silence of the woods, his mind idly wandering as he luxuriated in the warmth and peace of the camp. Aenor's body was delightfully soft and pliant as she rested up against his chest. The hand on her tummy began to move in an unconscious caress as the Maester sighed softly and pressed in closer to her.

Aenor's eyes flew open, her heart pounding in an unfamiliar rhythm as she felt the soft glide of his hand. Tension, or was it anticipation, began to hum along her form as she waited for... something.

Nothing. His breath began to settle into a regular cadence behind her. Aenor relaxed slowly, her vanity piqued. *Why, in Mira's name, isn't he trying anything? I don't know if I want to fool around with him but dammit, this is a little insulting!*

She was so wrapped up analyzing her desirability that she almost didn't feel his lips settle softly at the nape of her neck. But when she did, she stiffened up instantly, her thoughts screeching to a sudden halt. The lump in her throat instantly reformed as she swallowed slowly. It was time to decide.

Marius drew in her crisp scent slowly from the nape of her neck. It seemed so natural and so right in this place, to plant another soft kiss on her neck. This time, a slight flick of his tongue told him that she tasted as nice as she smelled. Then suddenly, he became aware that she had stiffened up and froze up himself. Time stopped as each waited for a sign from the other.

Aenor turned her head slightly to look over her shoulder, her head tilted up just enough to expose the length of her neck to his gaze. A silent invitation.

With a soft flash of hope and then a touch of triumph, Marius bent his head to taste her skin. Aenor arched her head back silently, her hands still demurely placed in front of her. Hesitantly, almost shyly, Marius planted soft, tantalizing kisses along the length of her neck, up along her jaw line until his lips were poised over hers. His gaze looked questioningly into hers as he waited for an answer.

Aenor lifted her head slightly to claim his lips in a gentle kiss. How odd, she thought. It had seemed such a momentous decision a moment ago, but now it seemed like a perfectly natural progression. She had expected an explosion of passion, but here was gentleness and a desire to linger. Nothing was going the way she had expected. Aenor freed her hands from under the furs to clasp his face as she kissed him thoroughly, her mouth exploring his curiously but in an unhurried manner. Strange, she though dimly, what's changed between us in the last week? When his arms slipped around her and his tongue slid into her mouth, she suddenly realized that she didn't need to figure that out right now.

One hand moved under the furs to trace the long length of his back. Under her light fingertips, his muscles shifted as he moved to deepen the kiss. No words yet, only the crackle of the fire beside them to keep them company. As their lips parted, Marius saw her eyes draw slowly open, her emerald gaze soft and misty. He drew in a silent breath. Suddenly all his secret desires seemed within reach. With a sudden sense of shock, he realized the feeling he had lived with for the past few decades could be summarized into one word: loneliness. He didn't love her but how could he possibly not want a woman who had brought unpredictability and wild adventure back into his life? When next he kissed her, it was with the giddy zest that suddenly swept through his soul.

Aenor gasped in surprise as his tongue plundered into her mouth with joyous abandon. Her hands came up to brace against his shoulders. An instant later, her brain clicked back on. Wait a minute! Passion! Thank the Gods, something I can understand! With a muffled laugh, she wrapped her arms around his neck and showed him how a warrior woman kisses.

He swung her over athletically until she was poised over him. Their furs shifted and tangled around them, effectively locking their legs into immobility. Darkly seductive eyes looked down into his, a tantalizing smile on red lips. His hands framed her face and slowly trailed down over her shoulders and between their bodies to cup her breasts. Living flesh warmed his hands through the fabric of her shirt. The Maester drew in a sudden shuddering breath as his eyes lingered on the soft swells under her leather shirt.

Aenor didn't make a move but continued to regard him with that inviting smile on her lips. His fingers, used to the delicate work of surgery, flowed down her shirt front, leaving a trail of metal snaps in their wake. At her waistband, he paused. In that moment, Aenor eased off him to sit back on his hips. Cold air rushed into the void left behind but he didn't feel a thing. All his reeling mind could concentrate on was the way her nipples suddenly thrust sharply up against the black leather of her shirt.

Slowly, Aenor drew the edges of her shirt apart, the dancing flames of the fire casting shifting shadows on her skin. Underneath, her breasts swelled up against black material, straining against the tight bodice she wore as support. She reached for the laces holding the edges together, but his hands stopped her. Silence reigned still as the Maester's fingers lingered over the laces, loosening them slowly, enjoying the way her skin revealed itself, the way her breasts filled out to poise themselves temptingly over him. Aenor lifted her hands slowly to her hair, her eyes never once leaving his as she undid her braid and drew her hands through the heavy, glowing mass of her hair. Then with that quiet, seductive smile of hers, she leaned forward invitingly, her hair slipping over her shoulders to fall about his face.

He attacked her with a predatory growl, arching up to bury his face between her breasts, his hands ripping away the last of her laces to free her upper body completely. A moment later, she was back on the ground as he rolled her over and poised himself over her. The fire quietly simmering in Aenor's veins flared suddenly into life as his mouth found a nipple. She gasped in satisfaction, her head going back and her fingers twining into his hair as she closed her eyes and gave herself up to the sensations. Sharp, delicious thrills darted from her nipple as his tongue rasped against it. She wanted to arch her hips against his, to encourage him to pleasure her but the furs binding them together wouldn't allow it. But that didn't stop him. His hands roamed with a will, fiercely cupping and squeezing her breasts before sweeping down to shape the curve of her hips. Then with a vivid curse, he broke away just enough to wrestle the furs trapping their legs. Next, a short spell set in place a shield that would keep their heat in and the cold out.

"Hold on," Aenor held him at bay with a hand planted on his chest as she realized what he had done. "Why haven't you been using that spell all this time? We could have saved ourselves a lot of frozen nights!"

"Big energy drain," he answered, as he started working at the laces on her breeches with dedication. "And the spell fades as soon as I fall asleep. Now, will you quit distracting me?"

Aenor put on a mock chastened look and propped herself up on both elbows as he worked, looking for all the world like a mermaid with her hair streaming about her and her lower body encased in black leather. She caught his gaze before letting her eyes drift lazily down his body. Marius paused, sitting over her with an intense look in his eyes.

"You are intoxicating..." he whispered with feeling. She smiled then, a simple mysterious smile. A moment later, Marius found himself being expertly undressed by a bare breasted woman with the knowledge of the ages in her eyes. The night was cold, but he didn't feel it. The blood rushing through his veins carried enough heat to keep him blazing.

Aenor's hands made short work of the snaps on his breeches, peeling them down his hips to reveal his swollen penis. She looked him over then, her gaze sliding down his body like the silent touch of a lover. Then he groaned softly between his teeth as a warm hand wrapped around the thickness of his cock. She moved up against him, close enough to tempt him into madness but with a challenging look in her eyes that discouraged him from bearing her down to the ground. Fingers slipped delicately around the head of his penis, spreading the moisture there tantalizingly. His hands came up to rest on her hips as he closed his eyes and concentrated on the pleasure of her touch.

Another warm hand wrapped around his shaft. Marius's eyes slid shut as he released his breath in delight. His reality suddenly shrank down into a single pulsing point of mindless pleasure as her palm swept firmly and evenly all over his sensitive head. Marius dropped his head forward in sinuous pleasure. Then the movement suddenly stopped, leaving him bereft.

Aenor had stiffened up in front of him, her eyes focused on a point beyond his left shoulder. Then she was moving in a blur, tumbling backwards to grab her sword sheath.

"Maester! Your magic!" she hissed as she sprang to her feet and steel hissed. With a single gesture, his magic shields clicked into place, shielding them both. He turned to see a man standing a few feet away, his hands tucked into his voluminous sleeves with an embarrassed expression on his face. The Maester whispered a short spell, clothing both he and Aenor with illusion. He came to his feet slowly, never taking his eyes off the intruder.

"Peace," said the black mage, his hands coming out to show they were empty.

"We've seen this one before," said Aenor tersely, gesturing toward the mage with the point of her sword.

151

Marius's eyes narrowed as a nagging image from his memory clarified.

"You were the first mage the Abida sent." The young mage nodded in response.

"I am the only one left," he stated flatly. "I'm here to discuss the details of the duel." Out of the corner of her eye, Aenor saw the muscles of the Maester's shoulders relax slightly. Assuming that he was prepared for whatever the black mage could do, she put her back to his and began to scan the woods for a surprise attack.

"My name is Regis, fourth year apprentice to the Abida," began the black mage. "It is an honor to meet you." The Maester bowed in return to the compliment.

"This is what the Abida proposes. The duel will occur outside the castle, administered by a neutral party. A wind elemental named Areas, is amenable to performing that office. I trust she is acceptable to you?" The Maester nodded, gesturing for the other man to continue.

"The rules of the duel will be the usual. A ring of 200 feet in radius. Neither combatant may step out of the ring without forfeiting the match. The match will continue either to the death or till one combatant yields. Also you may not approach the castle at any time, in any way."

"What about the stakes?" Marius interrupted. "This is the Abida's chance for vengeance. If I win, I want a promise that he will leave me in peace. Forever, in any land. I also want the secret to Agelessness." Regis shook his head.

"The first is acceptable, the second is not."

"Those are the conditions," replied the Maester implacably. "Take it or leave it." Regis stood a moment contemplating the man opposite him.

"I will need your promise that you will never let it fall in the hands of a mortal." Marius nodded.

"You have my word. Now, do I even have to ask what I forfeit if I lose?" The black mage frowned before a smile of genuine amusement crossed his lips at the hint of sarcasm in Marius's voice. Then his gaze turned on Aenor.

"Finally, the warrior may not accompany you." Aenor turned to face the intruder at that, a look of surprise on her face.

"That's ridiculous!" she stated incredulously. "You're asking him to step into enemy territory with no one to watch his back?"

"You have my word that no one will harm the Maester until he steps into the circle." Aenor shook her head in patent disbelief.

"We go together or not at all," she replied in a deadly voice.

The dark mage turned to face her fully, his eyes suddenly dark and commanding.

"Listen now, the both of you! You will not find Bodian unless the Abida allows it. And he will not allow it if unless you agree to these conditions. You will wander the mountains until you freeze to death or worse." The mage turned his dark eyes to Marius.

"My lord, there is no need to risk the warrior's life in this endeavor," he said quietly. "This has always been between you and the learned one and no one else should be involved. Bodian is a place for magic."

At that softly whispered warning, the Maester turned his head to look at Aenor with a peculiar look in his eyes. Aenor felt a sudden chill invade her heart as she read his thoughts as clearly as if he had said them aloud.

"I agree," said the Maester clearly, his eyes never once leaving Aenor's. His hand reached out and clamped onto the black mage's shoulder.

"Atira methka thiramon." Regis intoned in reply.

"No!" yelled Aenor as the two figures instantly began to shimmer and disintegrate. She threw herself towards them, trying to catch onto either of the figures, but it was already too late. She hurtled through the faint figures, crashing to the hard ground on the other side. They were already gone by the time she lifted herself onto one sore elbow and looked back over her shoulder.

Chapter 20

HEL! Her frustrated curse echoed through the silent mountains.

"The bastard!" Aenor swore to herself as she picked up her black leather shirt off the floor where she had abandoned it. When the Maester vanished, so did his spells. The cruel, cold wind had rushed around her without his protective barriers, chilling her bare skin so fast that it had taken on an almost bluish hue immediately. Did the bastard leave me here to freeze just so he could get to that renegade before I could? Aenor focused her mind on the one small part of her that was no longer completely hers.

Lya! I need you! She repeated the call, intensifying her concentration until she felt the dragon answer. She then pushed an image of her surroundings to Lya. Her lips spread slowly into a grim smile. Lya was coming for her. Few things could be hidden from a dragon's sight. Not when they operated on two planes.

The Dragonrider's Quest

She leant over to pick up her backpack. Her hand passed through its strap. Aenor startled, her shocked gaze fixed onto her hand as it began to sparkle and disintegrate. A moment later, the wind whistled hungrily through an empty camp.

A shaft of yellow light was the first thing that cut through the darkness of Aenor's world. She dropped to her knees, scrunching down while trying to regain her bearings. Beside her was a striped pole flying a red pennant and on her right, stretched a wide length of cream canvas. Aenor scrambled back silently on her hands and knees to get a better look. A tent sitting in the middle of a patchy field.

Fabric rustled and flapped in the strangely warm night as the tent glowed with the light from a dozen torches. Two shadows moved on the canvas wall, one plainly the Maester's. After judging that she wouldn't cast a shadow on the tent wall, Aenor shifted her bare sword into her left hand and crept quietly around to the tent flap. Pulling it a fraction of an inch open, she put her eye to it and looked through. The first things she saw were the Maester's eyes as he looked directly at her. His gaze remained carefully casual as it swept past her and around the tent as he talked and gestured at Regis with one hand. Aenor got the hint. She dropped the tent flap and retreated to the safety of the darkness beyond the circle of the torches.

Once safely hidden in the shadowy depths of a small grove of birches, Aenor allowed herself a quick pang of remorse for thinking him such a cur. It was such a cleverly done trick. Letting himself be brought into the Abida's territory, before porting her over to a familiar spot. She had talked to enough warrior mages to know that teleporting was a dangerous spell at best, and an insane one to try if one didn't know the physical layout of the destination. She had seen the writhing, distorted tree on the palace grounds that was reputed to be what was left of an apprentice. He had not studied his destination carefully enough before attempting the spell and rematerialized to himself melded into the trunk of a tree.

Lya! Aenor reached out with her mind. There was no response. *Lya!* Aenor tried again. *I've been moved. Somewhere south, because it's a lot warmer where I am. Try to follow my voice!* Aenor waiting, chilled at the lack of response from the dragon. *Could I have been moved out of range?*

A sudden motion at the tent's opening caught Aenor's eye. The black mage emerged from the tent, bowed formally to Marius and vanished slowly into the night. Without missing a beat, Marius dropped the flap of the tent before retreating into its depths. Biting her lip, Aenor dismissed the idea of sneaking over to him. She was in his realm now. He would have to make the first move. And he did. A few moments later, he emerged from the tent, walking over towards her grove, fumbling blatantly at his breeches. Aenor slipped quietly between the trees, heading to intercept him at the edge of the grove.

"Where's the castle?" she whispered from behind a tree as he stopped and fumbled some more with the flap of his breeches. He ignored her question as he settled down to the business of pretending to take a leak.

"The duel is at dawn tomorrow," he said in an undertone, religiously keeping his eyes glued to the ground

157

in front of him. "That would be the best time to get into Bodian. Everyone will be out front to watch the contest."

"I can't wait that long!" she hissed. "Now where in the abyss is the castle?"

"You'll see it in the morning," he answered cryptically, ignoring the intimidating glare she cast him. "Once this is all over, you'll need Lya to get you out of here. But you will need to go out to her. The wards around this place were created by Margary and are as strong now as when she was alive. Lya will be badly hurt if she tries to fly in." At that, he swiftly did up the snaps on his breeches. A slight chill ran down her spine, she suddenly realized what he was subconsciously saying to her.

"We're going to leave together," she stated quietly, her annoyance with him fading away to be replaced by cold trepidation.

His eyes lifted for the first time to look her straight in the eye. They had turned full-on silver, shining in their intensity. Aenor took a deep breath as the heat of his gaze touched her skin in an invisible caress.

"Take care of yourself," he whispered softly. And then he was gone.

Aenor stood stock-still while she tried to decide on her next move. As far as she could see, she had two choices. To comb the area right now, in the dark, to locate Bodian castle. There was a reason smart assassins attacked at night. But the truth of the matter was that she was exhausted after the day's hard ride. She knew she could infiltrate the castle if she really had to but she also knew perfectly well that tired people made bad mistakes. And she couldn't afford any of those. Her other choice: sleep till dawn and wing it.

She gritted her teeth. That would effectively give Marius the first shot at the Abida. Not the decision she longed to make but clearly the more intelligent one. A few moments later, Aenor found a fairly warm, dry hollow at the foot of a tree and curled up with her sword to catch a few hours of sleep.

Chapter 21

Aenor awoke just before the sun rose. Shaking loose leaves and dirt from her hair, she swiftly wove a few blades of grass into a rather flimsy back harness for her sword. After checking that her dagger was still safely in her boot, she slid through the underbrush of the woods. She was almost sure that she knew what she was doing.

Breaching the castle would be pointless at this stage because her quarry would soon be emerging for the duel. She hoped that the Abida had some nifty tricks up his sleeve because if the Maester didn't get him, she would. *First things first.* She had to acquire a long-range weapon. She sincerely doubted that she would be able to sneak up on the Abida in the middle of a wide, open field. *If only the Maester had teleported my bow along with me!*

Lya! Aenor pushed an image of the field to the dragon. It would be easy to see from the sky. There was still no response. *Perhaps the containment field interferes with our bond.*

160

Aenor paused to consider her situation. No castle to be seen anywhere. *Something is definitely off here.* She had originally thought that both she and the Maester had been teleported hundreds of miles south to a warmer zone, but that was nowhere near the truth. She had found the boundaries of this place they were in. A straight line marked where patchy grass gave way to sparse tundra vegetation and cold gray rocks. Across the expanse of grass, a bare granite cliff shot straight up for hundreds of feet. They weren't in some unnamed place far from their original location. They were still in the mountains, inside of some kind of containment bubble that held in warmth and kept the cold out.

Aenor had to admit she was very impressed with the scope of power on display here. Impressed and very disturbed. It had always been painfully obvious that she would not survive a face-to-face confrontation with the Abida, but now she was beginning to worry that Marius might not either. Just then, the sun appeared at the horizon line. Aenor glanced at it. Time to get back. The duel would be starting soon.

Aenor reached the field just as the first of the sun's weak rays spilled over the treetops and into the clearing. Keeping low among the underbrush, she didn't notice the transformation occurring in the middle of the field. As the sun's rays poured into the clearing, the air at the far end began to distort and shift like a mirror. Shimmering edges of a large object became visible as the angle of the sun's rays deepened with its rising. When Aenor finally looked up, the building had already mostly appeared. Her mouth dropped open as she gazed upon an ancient granite castle standing where nothing had stood a moment before. The heavy oak gates of the castle began to swing open with a loud creaking sound. She watched the Maester emerge from his tent, dressed in navy blue healer robes. He stood there, facing the castle, hands folded neatly in his sleeves, a calm look on his face.

What a beautiful day, thought the Maester, as he waited for his ancient nemesis to come forth to him. His mind was clear and focused. Dozens of memorized spells rested within him, ready to be unleashed. Still he didn't give in to the temptation to go over them once more. His life depended on his being alert, relaxed and in control. Far in front of him, two figures appeared under the arch of the castle's entrance. Regis, tall and youthful. And the Abida. The pair began walking across the field. Marius shook his head slightly. Like him, Ryce looked about twenty years older than when they had last met, but his limp was still in evidence. He dressed like a scholar, although the silver runes edging his black robes gave them the elegant formality appropriate for a mage duel.

A movement in Marius's peripheral vision caught his attention. He turned to see a six foot tall being, dressed in white gliding towards him with the gentle grace of a breeze. Bone white hair flowed unfettered to her waist, fluttering about as if stirred by wind. Her calm face radiated an ageless, unearthly beauty. The wind elemental named Areas, no doubt. She fixed him with an intense gaze, colorless eyes evaluating him silently. Marius bowed formally to her and was rewarded by a courtly nod.

The four met in the center of the clearing. For the first time in three hundred and fifty years, Marius found himself looking into the silver gray eyes of his teacher. Those same eyes bored back into his, coolly evaluating the man who had eluded him for so long. So intense was the moment that nobody noticed the lone figure that slipped through the oak gates of Bodian's curtain wall and into the castle proper.

"Marius. It has been a long time," said the Abida, his voice strangely vital for his age. "Welcome back to Bodian Castle." Marius bowed to the Abida.

"It is a pleasure to be here. And with an invitation too…" he finished with a touch of wry humor. A corner of the Abida quirked in an unwilling smile.

"Shall we begin?" came a beautifully mellow voice. Both mages turned towards the wind elemental.

"We all know the rules," Areas said calmly. "The first mage to step outside the circle forfeits." She raised one hand and a circle of fire suddenly sprang up around the group. "No magic may be directed outside the circle for any reason." Both she and Regis began to back out of the flaming circle. Both contestants retreated to put a safe distance between themselves. "The duel ends when one of the contestants is down." Marius and the Abida both glanced at each other at that.

"Begin!" Her voice resounded through the silent clearing.

Aenor reached for the massive bronze door of the castle's hall. She had realized that she would have to enter after all. If not to locate a bow, then to lie in wait for the Abida. Her heart thudded violently in her chest as her mind began to remind her of the mutants and booby traps that were rumored to protect the castle. *Oh well, I don't have much of a choice in the matter and the Maester is clearly tied up at the moment.*

The doors swung open easily with a firm push. In front of her loomed a wide corridor, dimly illuminated with flickering torches. Black puffs of smoke rose up from the torches to the high stone ceiling, leaving traces of soot on the stone gargoyles lining the walk. Aenor readied her sword, took a brave step over the lintel and waited. Nothing. Her breath expelled in a soft gust. Shifting into a cautious stance, she crept down the corridor, eyes shifting as she kept an eye out for surprises. Keeping her line of sight forward, Aenor never noticed the color transformation that began occurring among the stone gargoyles as she passed them.

The Maester's shields went up as soon as the duel began. Both combatants stood firm as they issued test mage bolts to gauge the strength of their opponent's shields. Blue lights sizzled and flickered over invisible barriers as the mage bolts were absorbed. The Abida's face was intense with concentration as he launched the first offensive.

"Akela tirana el!" he shouted, as he flung a corded pouch to the ground in front of him. The pouch spilled open, casting a wealth of powders and stones onto the grass. Instantly, the ground began to rumble and shudder as something rather large began to claw its way to the surface. The Maester didn't wait to see what it was. He had a pretty good idea what was coming and he swiftly came up with a counter attack. Under the cover of his shields, he spread his hands, palms down, and began to mutter under his breath, being careful to keep his strategy a secret from his opponent.

Then suddenly right in front of him, a gigantic earthen hand exploded from the ground with a hiss of steam. Marius gasped and stumbled as the violence of the creature's struggles loosened the ground beneath his feet. Even as the giant figure climbed out of the ground, he felt his own spell begin to move with greater urgency under his feet. The earth elemental loomed dangerously over him, one fist raised to smash him to the ground but then a fountain of water shot skywards from around its feet.

"Asana mehta!" yelled the Maester, darting back to escape from the earth elemental's assault. The water geyser drawn from the earth began to swirl around the earth elemental, faster and faster until it resembled a liquid tornado, eroding away the dirt body of the elemental. Wet clumps of earth began to pelt everybody within a two hundred foot radius of the whirlwind, prompting both Areas and Regis to bring up their shields. The Abida realized the pointlessness of that tactic and released his hold on the elemental, which promptly collapsed to the ground as a heap of wet mud. Marius barely had time to drop into a roll as a large fireball came hurtling at him, its passage echoed by a sonic boom. With that dramatic opening, the duel swung into full combat mode.

Chapter 22

Aenor was in real trouble. She didn't have time to react to the whistling that signaled the deadly attack of the gargoyles. She cried out as sharp claws raked through her leather shirt and into the skin of her shoulders. She dropped into a roll, neck craned skywards to see a creature from ancient myth soar silently into the heights of the great corridor. She had barely time to regain her balance before another monster shot towards her, claws extended, screaming a harsh challenge as its leathery wings sent powerful currents swirling around her. Aenor didn't stop to think. Her sword swung and crackled violently against one wing. Claws scraped harmlessly past her torso as the impact knocked the creature aside, sending it crashing into the opposing wall. It crumpled to the floor shrieking, with one wing snapped and flapping uselessly.

The corridor behind her was lined with struggling figures as pair after pair of gargoyles fought their way out of their ancient imprisonment. Another wave of creatures came free and swept a deadly trail down the corridor towards their prey. Aenor muttered a silent prayer as she turned tail and ran for her life.

The end of the corridor swept up towards her as deadly claws and teeth snapped about her. She raced through the open archway, before throwing herself against its heavy wooden doors, straining to close them against the invasion of deadly fliers. Two gargoyles managed to sweep through the gap before she forced the doors shut, arm muscles straining against the power of the creatures screaming and flapping on the other side. Claws reached through the narrow gap and raked across her face and hair. She gasped from the pain as blood from the scratches trickled into her eyes and into her mouth. Straining madly, she forced the doors shut and bolted them. Then suddenly, a sharp-toothed mouth sank into her arm from behind. She screamed in pain, as she was shoved face first into the hard wood of the door. That was when the warrior in her broke free.

She spun around, eyes blazing as she yelled her war cry. The fliers backstroked thoughtfully as they regarded her silently, their red eyes burning in their animalistic faces. Aenor's sword came forward, her dagger slipping easily into her left hand. She crossed blades in a defensive stance and then placed her back against the door.

"Come on then, you bastards." she goaded softly. They came. Air whistled as they attacked simultaneously. Aenor's sword drove forwards, cutting through the air unerringly as it pierced one gargoyle through the breast. The impact never even slowed her down as she forced the sword onwards in its swing, knocking its victim into the other flier and up against the wall. The weight of the shrieking gargoyle pinned on her sword dragged the point of her sword down then, but that was easily remedied when she dislodged the dying creature with one booted foot. The gargoyle flopped to the floor, arms and wings flapping violently as it went into its death throes. The remaining flier picked itself off the floor and launched itself into the air, circling above Aenor warily.

With her sword at the ready, Aenor began to back away into the next room, keeping a steady eye of the flapping creature above her. With a quick swipe, she wiped away the blood dripping into her eyes, leaving a deep red swath across her face. Numerous cuts and slashes on her body oozed blood, draining her strength slowly. But there was still a lot of fight left in her. She just needed to find a long-range weapon. With a sudden burst of speed, Aenor dashed into the next room. The flier drew in its wings at the unexpected move, dropped into a high-speed dive, only to smash into the heavy wood door she slammed into its face. It slid slowly to the floor with a whimper, leaving a wet sticky trail of fluid on the dark rich wood of the door.

On the other side, Aenor sagged weakly against the warm wood, gasping for breath. Then suddenly her muscles cramped convulsively. She staggered up against the door. An unpleasant suspicion began to form in her mind. The strange sensations she was experiencing couldn't just be due to her loss of blood.

"No," she breathed, her head dropping back against the door in realization. *Poison…*

Marius was face to face with a dread wolf. Its eyes were dancing flames, its maw dripping with froth and gore. A dread wolf's bite was death but that was decidedly pleasant compared to its breath. The Maester choked as the stench from the wolf's decaying jaws swept towards him.

With a swift incantation, Marius summoned flames to his fingertips and sent it surging towards the undead creature. Its fur caught fire like dry tinder, but that didn't even slow it down. It sprang into a leap, its dripping fangs reaching for his flesh. Marius sidestepped before sending it out of the circle with a well-placed boot. The creature was instantly sent back to its own plane as its body went past Areas's containment fields.

Marius turned on the ball of his foot and pointed towards the Abida's feet. The ground opened up beneath the Abida at a single word of command. The black mage dropped into the smoking fissure with a yell, just managing to catch hold of the edge of the crevice with one hand. The Abida's feet scrabbled furiously against the rocky side of the fissure, trying to gain a foothold. A short distance beneath him rushed an underground river, the water steaming and bubbling with heat. Marius strode to the side of the crevice, looking down at his struggling opponent, one hand outstretched to cast a mage bolt. But something stopped him. A memory of himself preaching to a roomful of apprentices. *Healers do not take life. We protect it.* With a strangely twisted look, Marius stepped away to give the Abida some room.

A moment later, the Abida levitated himself out of the fissure and came to rest back on solid ground. His robes settled around him as the fissure behind him closed with a single gesture. The black mage had a thoughtful look on his face but he didn't say a word. Instead he nodded to the sylph elder who gestured for the duel to continue. Marius flashed off a fireball to cover his next move. As the flames flowed over the Abida's shields, the Maester dropped to his hands and knees.

"Menelaya ikmi thella may," Marius whispered, as he bent the power of his mind to his will. Marius gasped as pain exploded into his consciousness. Muscles screamed and twisted. Bones shortened, nails grew, hair sprouted like tendrils of grass. When the smoke and flames cleared from the circle, there was only a single human within the circle. Standing across from the Abida, crouched an oversized black panther. With a twitch of its powerful tail, the cat launched itself at the coughing mage.

Aenor ran through the maze of corridors looking for the grand hall. *Every castle has a great hall and every great hall is decorated with weapons. It's practically a rule.* She heaved a huge sigh of relief when she stumbled through an archway and into a deserted room. The scrape of her steel shod boots on the stone floor echoed through the cavernous hall as she skidded to a halt. Around her was a dazzling, though rather dusty, display of weaponry. As she struggled to force air into her laboring lungs, Aenor's eye fell upon the very thing she was after. A silver bound bow hung high up on a wall, complete with a quiver of arrows. She laughed out loud in triumph. The adrenalin pumping through her body surged, suppressing the effects of the poison in her bloodstream for just a little longer.

She trotted to the far wall when the bow hung and made a leap for it. Her fingertips came within a few inches of one end but they slid away a moment too soon. Frustrated, she looked around for a chair she could use and that was when she noticed the mutant watching her. It stood behind her, a cat-like creature about half her height but standing on its hind legs like a human. The lean sweep of its well-developed muscles was accentuated by the short dark fur covering its body. It just stood there, tail swinging as it regarded her silently.

Aenor turned slowly to face it, one hand going over her shoulder to draw her sword. The cat-creature moved like a sudden flash of lightning, springing at her without any warning. Aenor yelled in fear as she threw herself to the ground and rolled away as fast as she could. She leapt to her feet, her right calf getting ripped by a set of sharp claws as she sprang away from the creature. Running, she made for the only piece of furnishing in the room. Faded, floor length draperies that swooped down in each corner of the hall.

Running at full speed, she launched herself into the air and slammed into the swags. Her hands clutched at the faded material convulsively as she began hauling herself up the cloth pillar. Beneath her, she could hear the material shred as the cat creature tried to follow her up the drapes. With a sense of elation, she realized that the creature's

172

claws gave it limited purchase as they only shredded the fragile fabric. The creature started to snarl furiously as she reached the top of the drapes and perched there like a roosting pigeon.

It was fairly hard not to notice the rope that was attached to the clip buried in the wall. She followed the length of fiber to the large central chandelier that hung in the middle of the great hall. A tired grin formed on her face. Here was her chance to enact that iconic scene bards loved to sing about. The part where the hero swung dramatically across a crowded room on such a rope to land safely on the other side. There was an appropriate balcony across from her, but everything else was completely wrong.

The chandelier was at least twice her weight, which would mean that it would start dropping as soon as she untied the rope. The best she could hope for was to swing aimlessly in the middle of the hall as the rope she was using shrunk to half its original length. Looking down at the cat creature, that was starting to work itself into a frenzy below her, she decided to go for it anyway.

She began doubting the wisdom of her choice just as soon as the rope unraveled in her hands and drew taut. The chandelier began falling, catapulting her into the air. Too late now! Aenor lifted her legs forward to add momentum to the swing, just as the rope began to shorten dangerously. Then at the high point of her first swing, she closed her eyes and let go of the rope. Air whizzed by her for almost an eternity. And then she slammed stomach first into the heavy wooden banister of the balcony she was aiming for. With a soft, heartfelt groan, she doubled up over the dark wood of the banister and slowly tumbled over to the hard floor waiting on the other side.

As she stood up, clutching her aching abdominals, her eyes fell upon a cobweb covered crossbow displayed on the back wall of the balcony. She whispered fervent thanks to Mira as she lifted the heavy instrument from its holders and examined it closely. In its spare bolt holder, rested a single rusty bolt, ready to be fired.

The Maester's heavy feline body slammed the Abida to the floor. To his credit, the black mage didn't even shriek as he saw the set of razor sharp fangs snarling over his face. The cat placed one heavy paw on the Abida's windpipe and began to press down in a move he had seen Aenor use before. The Abida's hands clutched vainly at the paw, as he began to struggle and gasp for air. A feral though understandable word emerged from the cat's jaws.

"Yield."

"No!" gasped the Abida, as his body began to flail beneath the cat's. The pressure on his windpipe intensified.

"Yield." No answer. The Abida's face began to turn blue. Marius realized that Ryce would rather go to his grave before submitting to a former student. He lifted his paw off the Abida's throat.

"Centuries ago, you spared my life out of fairness and honor. Today, I repay that debt. We are even." Ryce sat up, sucking down deep breaths of air and shook his head, still unable to speak.

Up high on the castle battlements, Aenor took aim at the Abida with the crossbow she had found. She swore softly as her sight blurred and twisted. Her hands were clammy, cold sweat dripped into her eyes and her muscles were trembling uncontrollably. The adrenaline rush that had slowed the poison's progress had faded and so had its healing effects. She focused her mind, willing her weakness to fade. One shot. That was all she had.

Aenor! A golden voice called in her mind.

Lya! Thank Mira, you're here. I'm in real trouble.

I can't get through this invisible wall. What should I do?

Right now, I need some of your strength!

Suddenly, Aenor felt a warm infusion of raw energy spread throughout her body. Her hands stopped trembling, her sight line cleared momentarily as she focused in on the black clad figure sitting in the middle of the field. Her finger tightened on the crossbow's trigger as she targeted her victim. She didn't see the Maester's head suddenly swivel in her direction. She couldn't see his eyes widen as he saw her leaning over the battlements with some sort of weapon in her hands. All she knew was the moment when the bolt left the crossbow with a resonant sound, and the wonderful sense of peace that overcame her when she realized that her shot was perfect. The crossbow slid from her nerveless finger, falling hundreds of feet to the cobblestones below, as she sagged unconscious to the floor.

"Gods!" swore the Maester as he flung his hand to bring up his shield. The rusty bolt hit the shield, flattening into a misshapen disk before dropping into the grass a few feet away from Marius's feet. The Abida had twisted around at his adversary's yell, just in time to see the warrior maid on his battlements collapse. Overhead, the shrill scream of a dragon in flight cut through the air as flames billowed over his containment shield, tracing it in lines of fire.

His gaze came back to Marius, eyes burning with anger. "You brought the warrior with you!" he spat out, his voice vibrating with fury. "You broke the rules! You forfeit!"

"I spared your life. Twice," stated the Maester baldly, meeting the Abida's gaze calmly. Regis and Areas glanced at each other, seeing an opening.

Up above them, Lya swept in for another attack. Aenor was fading. She slammed into Bodian's protective shields to no avail. Screaming in fury, she pounded the wards with flame and then the strength of her own body, hoping to break through. Below her, several figures were in deep conversation when suddenly one of them looked up and raised his hand.

Lya, on her next attack, found herself flying through the barrier and into the Abida's realm. The group watched the approach of the dragon with growing concern.

"It's not slowing down," muttered Regis. "Oh, Hel." Everyone scattered like ants. Everyone except Marius. He stood his ground as the dragon drove straight down towards him. His nerve almost failed him as he realized just how fast she was going, but he clung tenaciously to the belief that Lya would not intentionally harm him. Then with a sudden sense of horror, Marius realized that she wasn't going to stop and began to crouch. Talons uncurled and spread wide above him. He yelled as they grabbed hold of his shoulders and yanked him off the ground.

Wind whistled by him as Lya raced towards the castle. Marius tried to calm himself enough to take control of the dragon's mind, but he was too flustered to succeed. Then there was no time. He lifted his arms instinctively to protect his face as the cold, gray walls of the castle came at him. One second he was in a dragon's clutches, the next he was airborne and in the third, he was hitting a very hard stone floor.

He lifted his head groggily to see Aenor sprawled out in an ungainly position a few yards away from him. He lifted his aching body and crawled over to her. His eyes narrowed as he noted her clammy skin. The healer in him emerged with full force.

"Aenor! What have you done to yourself?"

Chapter 23

The next few days were a string of sounds and sensations for Aenor as her body fought to live. Hands feeding her broth. Occasional infusions of energy that gave her body the strength to sweat out the poison. The murmur of voices as she was sponged down with wonderfully cool water. And purging, a whole lot of purging.

When Aenor finally regained her senses, she opened her eyes to find a candle burning beside her bed. She squeezed them shut immediately; her eyes too sensitive even for that dim light. Her body ached with a dull throb, her head pounded and the taste in her mouth was absolutely vile. She was clothed in a thin linen chemise, which had clearly been through a lot.

Parting her eyelids just a little, she let them adjust for a minute. Slowly, she lifted her head with an effort to look around the room. She was in a windowless chamber, with only a brazier to hold back the chill of the granite walls.

The Maester jerked up in his chair beside her when he detected her movement.

"How do you feel?" he asked softly, as he sat down on the edge of the bed.

"Horrible…" she croaked. "Can I have some water?" He nodded and reached for a pitcher of water.

"A little of the poison is still in your bloodstream," he said, as he propped her up and held a glass of water to her mouth. "I drew as much of it out as I could. You should feel a lot better tomorrow."

"What happened after I passed out?" she asked, as he lowered her back down to her pillows.

"The Abida and I have agreed to put the past behind us and move on."

"So the Abida still lives. I failed."

"You didn't fail, Aenor. Your shot would have felled him had I not stopped it."

Aenor's eyes widened in disbelief. "You interfered?"

The Maester sat back down on the bed and took hold of her hand. "I prevented an unnecessary death," he corrected carefully. "Things had taken a positive turn when you fired off that shot." She shook her head in disgust.

"Am I a prisoner now?" she asked flatly.

"You are a guest," he stated firmly. "We may stay until you're fit for travel."

"Then what?"

"Then we leave."

"No, this isn't finished." Aenor replied in a tight voice. "He's still a danger to my country."

"Believe me, he is not!" said Marius, leaning forward urgently. "The Abida has never been interested in politics or power. He won't aid Taren in any way. He only wanted me and his collaboration with Taren was a one-time affair. Let it go!" Aenor looked back at him evenly, but the intent in her eyes was answer enough. Marius sat back with a resigned look.

"For your own safety, don't challenge him here. He's out of your league."

"Well, I'm not in great shape, so I suppose that I don't have much of a choice right now. Where's Lya?"

"She's outside. Probably hunting. She's been bringing in meat for the castle as our contribution while we stay. That's a savvy dragon you're bonded to." Aenor smiled limply.

"So what kind of bargain did you strike with the Abida?" asked Aenor, changing the subject not very subtly.

"Nothing earth shaking. We're going to go our separate ways. He now accepts that I don't have the secret to Agelessness and that has relaxed him somewhat. I'm never to return here, but that's an easy constraint for me to accept. He hasn't done much to improve the place," quipped Marius with a fake shudder.

"So it's back to Huria for you?"

Marius nodded. "It will be a little uncomfortable now, if word has gotten out that I've engaged in fights and duels. Healers are not supposed to practice violence. The faculty may request that I step down. Or they may not. I have no idea. It would be a loss to me as the college is home now. But at the core of things, I believe in putting good out into the world, whether it be as a healer or as an educator. I'll find a way to use my talents for that. Perhaps I'll travel to the east and learn their methods. I have time on my side, after all," he finished with a grin.

Aenor looked at him evenly from her bed. Then a tentative smile spread slowly over her lips.

"Then I am happy for you," she said quietly. "You know your path."

"If you ever feel like leaving the guard," added the Maester archly. "I could use someone to watch my back." Aenor chuckled, wincing as her abused innards protested.

"You do that well enough on your own. And my path lies with the guards."

Marius nodded with a smile. "I know. Do you think you can handle some solid food?" Aenor's stomach clenched and she must have blanched because he added. "Broth, then. Lya brought in a nice deer yesterday."

The next day, Aenor actually felt human when she awoke, alone in her chamber. She sat up in bed cautiously, her abused body aching faintly. Lya?

Welcome back to the land of the living, replied Lya. For a while there, I wasn't sure you would.

Are you all right?

Yes, I'm right outside the castle, resting beside a hot spring. Lya pushed an image of a wide pool ringed with dark rocks. *You should come to me.*

Aenor perked up immediately. A bath sounded heavenly. Days of sickness had taken its toll on her and she felt positively rank. She swung her feet to the floor and gingerly got to her feet. An inspection of the single cabinet in the room, revealed her mercenary leathers and clean small-clothes folded neatly, along with a few extra chemises and bath supplies. Heaven.

Aenor slipped into a chemise, flung her furs over it and armed herself with towel and soap. Swinging open the heavy door of her chamber, she found herself in a corridor with light at the end. Heading towards the light, she found a door to the exterior and entered the courtyard of the castle. It was still early in the day, the air chilly like a spring morning. Navigating with Lya's help, she made her way outside the curtain wall of the castle. Once outside, Lya was clearly visible as she had reared onto her hind legs, turning herself into a large blue signpost.

Aenor picked her way through the scrubby ground towards Lya. Although she felt miles better, her legs felt weak and unsteady over the uneven terrain. Dropping her supplies by the side of the pool she went to greet Lya, who lowered her snout to sniff her in diagnosis.

You'll need another day here, stated Lya glumly. *You don't smell of poison but your guts are still inflamed.*

Aenor nodded in thanks and turned back to the pool. It was a fair size, ringed with granite boulders. Steam rose from the crystal clear water and it smelt faintly metallic.

It's perfectly safe, stated Lya. *I've been drinking from it. Tastes awful, but it works.*

Aenor stuck a toe in. Definitely on the hot side but bearable. She pulled the chemise over her head and waded in hip-deep, winching from the heat. She lay back to float in the water, letting the water loosen up her limp hair. Floating her way back to the edge of the pool, she sat up and starting soaping her hair.

Have you seen the Abida since the mage duel? Aenor asked, as she ducked under the water to rinse out her hair, bubbles gently floating away to form a ring around her.

Once. I've seen him walking the grounds with the Maester. Aenor surfaced and wiped the water of her eyes, thinking hard. So, the two mages had reconciled. It confirmed what Marius had told her the previous day.

Aenor, there is something else here, said Lya hesitantly. *Something very old and very powerful. Magical, I think. We should leave as soon as you are able.*

Aenor twisted around in the water to look at Lya. Dragons by nature, operated on multiple planes and could sense things that humans couldn't. Are you sensing the Abida's power?

No, I recognize his signature, and the Maester's. This feels different.

Lya suddenly lifted her head. *The Maester is on his way here,* she warned. Aenor turned her head but saw nothing. When Marius reached the pool, she was busy lathering up her shoulders with soap.

"Good morning, Aenor," he said, a little surprised. "You must be feeling a lot better."

"I am, my lord. It feels good to be up. Please feel free to join me in the pool," she invited a tad formally, as she swept the hot water over her shoulders, little soap bubbles floating about her.

Marius nodded at her in thanks and stripped down before slipping into the pool a few feet away from her. He let out a deep sigh and leant back against a rock to relax. Aenor got to her feet to work the soap down the rest of her body. Marius regarded her with a healer's eye. Expelling the poison had burned off what little fat she had, leaving her a little gaunt. Her movements were smooth and controlled so there was probably no muscle or nervous damage. *All in all, there will be no long-term damage,* he thought in satisfaction.

If Aenor's skin had not already turned red from the heat, she would have flushed from his inspection. She sank back down into the pool to wash the soap away and felt a little more shielded. There was a new awkwardness between them that was regrettable, but their paths no longer aligned so perhaps that was for the best.

"Would you like me to scrub your back?" he asked. After a slight hesitation, she nodded and moved closer, handing over the soap and turning to present her back, bringing up her knees to her chest and wrapping her arms around them.

"You're doing really well. We should be able to leave in a couple of days." He continued in a matter-of-fact voice, as he moved the wet tendrils of her hair over her shoulders to expose her back.

She has definitely lost too much weight, he thought. The shape of her vertebra and ribs showed a little clearly through her skin, lending her a fragility that didn't normally exist. Being this close to a naked woman in a warm bath was normally a forerunner to a pleasant interlude, but right now Marius felt protective rather than amorous, as he lathered his hands and applied them to her back.

"Are you certain that the Abida is not going to interfere in the war?" she turned her head and asked over her shoulder.

"I am," he replied with certainty. Aenor relaxed and allowed herself to enjoy the hypnotic movement of his hands on her back.

"All right then, we'll leave tomorrow," she said decisively, finally giving up on the assassination idea. "I can recover just as well at home." Behind them, Lya stirred in anticipation as she caught the gist of Aenor's thoughts.

"Fair enough. You are doing remarkably well and Lya will be doing the hard work, after all." Marius frowned. There were quite a few knots in between her shoulder blades. He pressed down with his thumbs, alternating pressure on and off, to loosen them. In front of him, Aenor let her head fall forward onto her knees, giving herself over to the warmth of the water and the pleasure of his hands.

So, are you going to mate with him now? came Lya's voice in Aenor's head. Aenor's head shot up.

Of course not, she sputtered mentally. I'm half dead over here and, anyway, I wouldn't do such things in front of you.

It doesn't matter if it's in front of me or not. I'll know it regardless. Like that time a few nights ago when you were enjoying him.

You were listening in? Aenor was torn between horror and titillation.

It wasn't so much listening in, as being broadcasted to, replied Lya matter-of-factly. You were a little loud.

Aenor subsided in embarrassment. She had gone through a similar situation when Eld mated for the first time. Broadcasting was an understatement.

Don't feel bad, Lya replied soothingly, finally realizing that human were more sensitive about mating than dragons. *We're bonded. You'll live through it with me when I become old enough to mate. If it makes you feel better, don't do it in front of me. I understand, although it really would be quite educational.*

Aenor dropped her head forward again with a groan. Misunderstanding, Marius lessened the pressure of his thumbs and then laved the warm water over her back to keep her skin warm in the cool air. Eventually, Aenor lifted her head up and stretched.

"Would you like me to do you? Your back, I mean." Aenor mentally smacked her forehead, before turning around to face Marius. A corner of his lips had quirked up.

"That would be much appreciated," he replied as he leaned over to pluck the soap off the rock edge to hand to her. Spinning around with a wave of water, he presented his back to her. Marius kept his thoughts virtuously fixed on the future as he felt her slippery hands slide over him. He enjoyed her touch (like any healthy male would) but they would be parting soon and it would be best not to entangle himself with her any further.

Aenor was thinking much along the same lines as she worked the soap over his shoulders and back. Now that Lya had brought up that night by the campfire, it was firmly stuck in her mind. She considered it a blessing that that idiot apprentice had interrupted them that night, as sex would only have complicated their association. *Ships in the night, that's what we should be,* Aenor lectured herself. Even as Aenor lectured herself on keeping to the straight and narrow, she unconsciously leaned in to get closer to him, the tips of her breasts brushing his back as she ran the soap over him, somewhat unnecessarily by this point.

Marius felt the light touch of her nipples on his back and squeezed his hands into fists, wrestling his thoughts away from the touch of her hands on his body. *Gods, Aenor has just risen from her sick bed!* Her hands slid over his shoulders and down a little way down his chest. Behind them, Lya snorted in amusement, which broke the moment.

187

Marius caught her hand with one of his and looked over his shoulder at Aenor.

"We can't do this, Aenor," he stated flatly. "We have no future together, by your own will."

Aenor jerked her hand back, a little stung. "I know that. Getting involved now would be utter foolishness. Plus, I'm far from my best right now."

Marius turned in the water slowly to face her.

"Don't mistake me, Aenor," he said softly, trying to avoid wounding her pride. "You are a *very* desirable woman, and we both know there is an attraction between us. Just as we both know that it won't lead anywhere." *My life will keep going while yours will fade.* The additional complication hung between them wordlessly.

Aenor nodded in acceptance, her face reddening, as she withdrew to her end of the pool. To defuse the embarrassment of the situation, she quickly changed the subject. "By the way, Lya senses another magical presence here. A powerful one."

Marius frowned. "There's no one else here except for Ryce, Regis and myself. The elemental has left the grounds."

Lya volunteered more information. *Tell him that it's definitely not human.*

"She says the presence isn't human," repeated Aenor obediently.

Marius twisted in the water towards Lya, peering over the rocky rim to address her directly. "Perhaps you sense the ley lines here," he said confidently.

Aenor glanced over at Lya to check if she knew what those were and got a mental shrug in return. "What are ley lines?" Aenor asked, on Lya's behalf.

"Ley lines are sources of natural energy deep underground," Marius explained, unconsciously slipping into his teaching voice. "Margary told me that two ley lines cross here at Bodian Mountain and are responsible for the hot springs that heat the castle. Their natural energy is what drew her to Bodian in the first place. She was working on a way to tap their power. I can't sense the ley lines, but I suppose it's possible that Lya can."

I suppose that could be it, Lya said hesitantly. *But it still doesn't feel right. We should definitely leave this place as soon as possible.*

Aenor's stomach rumbled softly then, notifying her that it was finally up to solid food. Aenor excused herself and got to her feet, wading over to where she had left her clothes. Marius politely averted his eyes and continued his own ablutions, while Aenor toweled off and got dressed.

"First thing in the morning then?" asked Marius from the pool.

Aenor glanced at him and nodded.

The next day, Aenor clattered down the stone stairs in full mercenary regalia. The weapons left at their mountain campsite had been returned to her and were once again strapped in place. Outside in the bright morning light, Lya waited impatiently to fly. Marius and the Abida were waiting for her at the foot of the stairs.

"My lords." she bowed slightly, flicking her eyes to the Abida.

"I have to say it's been interesting, warrior," the Abida said pointedly. "I can hardly believe I sheltered a woman who was trying to kill me. Am I safe in your presence?"

"My queen would like to know if you are a threat to her realm, my lord," Aenor stated plainly.

"I couldn't care less about her realm. As long as her subjects leave me and mine in peace, we have no issues."

"Will you put that in writing?"

Marius held out a scroll. "He already has."

Aenor took it and unrolled it. It read 'Leave me alone and I'll leave you alone. - The Abida.'

Nonplussed, Aenor asked a clarifying question "Are you saying that you will not take sides in the war, nor interfere in any way?"

"Absolutely," replied the Abida, waving one hand negligently. "I have no interest in politics. I'm on the verge of an amazing breakthrough and I'll be focusing on that." The Abida looked like he had already mentally moved on so Aenor decided to leave it at that.

"Shall we go, Aenor?" Marius asked. *With pleasure, she thought.*

"Thank you for your hospitality, my lord," Aenor said, as she clamped one hand on her sword hilt and bowed gracefully to Abida. With a nod to the Maester, she turned and strode out of the castle courtyard.

Marius turned to face his former teacher. "Farewell Ryce," said Marius quietly. "I wish you well."

"Likewise," replied the Abida stiffly, before extending one hand. "You've grown into a good man, Marius.' They briefly shook hands before Marius turned to follow Aenor.

"Don't come back," came a reminder over his shoulder. Marius smiled to himself and kept walking.

Chapter 24

Aenor headed back to her quarters at a brisk walk, dressed in her navy uniform, with Tamar by her side. She had just made her report to the queen. Her Majesty had taken the Abida's scroll, read the single line on it and had gravely handed it to her secretary to be filed. It would be taken to the archives and stored in the treaties section.

"You did well on this mission, Aenor," said Tamar gruffly, as she strode along beside Aenor. "You may not have killed the Abida, but you used good judgment in dealing with him. If he honors his side of the bargain, we will too."

"Thank you, Aunt," responded Aenor in a distracted voice. In the meeting, the queen had also informed her that the Maester was due to be escorted back to Huria tomorrow, but not by her. She was to stay and get integrated with the Prince's Guard.

"You're thinking about the Maester's departure, aren't you?" asked Tamar, with great perception. "You've always known that he would have to return to Huria."

"Yes, I've always known," replied Aenor flatly.

"Well, speak of the devil," murmured Tamar, her eyes fixed on the figure ahead of them. Standing in front of Aenor's door, was the Maester himself. Marius had been commandeered by the Hurian ambassador upon his return to Miramar and had been staying at the embassy. They hadn't seen much of him since then.

"Well met, Maester" said Tamar once they reached him. "I hear that you are leaving us tomorrow."

Marius favored Tamar with a faint smile. "I am indeed. I'm using my final hours in Miramar to say farewell to my friends here."

Tamar extended her hand for a firm handshake. "You have done Norwall a great service, my lord. We won't forget it." With a quick half-bow, Tamar headed off to her own quarters, leaving Aenor and Marius staring awkwardly at each other.

"Would you like to come in for a drink?" began Aenor hesitantly.

"I'm afraid that I can't," Marius replied. "The ambassador is hosting a farewell dinner for me this evening and I have to head back for that."

"I see. Well, I suppose that this is it then." Following her aunt's lead, Aenor extended her hand. Instead of shaking it, Marius caught her hand and lifted it to his lips in an old-fashioned gesture. Aenor caught her breath, as his lips brushed gently over the back of her hand.

"Farewell, Aenor Merivel," said the Maester in a soft voice. "It has been a great pleasure knowing you. I hope that we meet again in happier circumstances."

Aenor struggled to find her voice. "I wish you a safe journey home, my lord," she replied, working hard to keep her voice even.

With a crooked smile, Marius took his leave and walked away. Aenor turned, keeping her eyes on him until he turned a corner and disappeared from view. Turning back in an abrupt motion, she unlocked her door and disappeared into her chamber.

Late that night, as Marius was relaxing in his room after his farewell dinner, a loud knock at the door disturbed his reverie. At his door was a footman, with Aenor standing close behind him.

"I'm sorry to disturb you, my lord. This guard is here with an urgent message from the queen." The footman stepped out of the way, gesturing Aenor into the room.

This can't possibly be good, Marius thought with dread, as he eyed Aenor. She must have been roused from her bed to deliver this message, as her uniform looked hastily fastened and her hair unbound. Aenor silently held out a scroll wound with decorative cord. Marius took it from her, dismissed the servant with a nod and closed his bedroom door as the footman departed.

He turned to face Aenor, a frown on his face. "Do you know what this is about?" he lifted the scroll.

"More or less." Aenor took a deep breath, plucked the scroll from his hand and dropped it on the plush rug beneath their feet. "I've decided that I would like a proper goodbye." Screwing up her courage, she stepped up to him, hoping that he wouldn't reject her again. She wound her arms around his neck and pulled his face down for a kiss.

When they broke apart, Marius had to ask. "Are you sure, Aenor? This hasn't gotten any smarter since the *last* time we almost had sex."

Aenor relaxed and chuckled deep in her throat. "Definitely not. But life is short, and we still have unfinished business between us."

Marius's heard started to pound heavily in his chest at her words. "I *have* been thinking of that night in the wilderness," he murmured, sliding one hand into the mass of hair at her nape and drawing it forward over her shoulder. "And fantasizing about your hair draped over me. I'm glad that you've resisted the urge to cut it like all the other female warriors. It makes you different, yet no less strong." Aenor swallowed, silenced unexpectedly by the sincerity in his voice.

"I don't need promises or fine words, Marius. Tonight, I just want you."

195

Her whispered admission set fire to his blood. Even though Aenor had denied any need for words, Marius needed to make this night more than just a meaningless romp between the sheets. Pulling away slightly, he drew Aenor over to the full-length looking glass propped in a corner of the room. He then stepped behind her so that he was looking over her shoulder at both their reflections.

Marius wrapped an arm around Aenor's waist to hold her tight against his body while his other hand came up to draw back her hair from her neck. At a tiny little bite on her neck, Aenor gasped and watched her nipples harden and show through two layers of fabric. His lips left her neck to whisper into her ear.

"I want to remember you like this," his voice rumbled by her ear. The vibration of his voice by her ear triggered delicious shivers running down her sides. One finger outlined the delicate shape of her lips softly.

"Your hair and your body..." he whispered against her ear. Reaching from behind her, he unsnapped the front of her navy top and pulled it off her shoulders, leaving her in her tightly laced linen bodice. "Your body that makes my mind reel."

Marius lifted one hand to her neck and swept it slowly down to shape the curve of one breast and then further down over her hip. His fingers found the snap at her waist and her pants dropped to the floor to puddle around her ankles. "Beautiful, strong, loyal, desirable, that's the way I'll remember you." Aenor flushed hot, her heart banging away in her chest like a trip hammer. She had come here to seduce him, but somehow the tables had turned.

She twisted around to face him, her fingers finding the buttons on his tunic as he held back and let her work. His tunic hit the floor. His breeches were next as he backed her towards the bed. They fell on the firm bed in a tangle of limbs, but he bounced back up a moment later because his boots were in the way of his breeches. Boots came off, then breeches, then small-clothes and all was right in the world again. He turned and drew himself up against her side.

Aenor lay back onto her bed still clad in her small-clothes, her lashes coming down to veil her eyes as she let her gaze wander over his body. Her hands found his shoulders, her fingertips tracing the shape of the muscles beneath. He leant over her, letting her touch his body to her heart's content. He gasped softly when her nails scratched lightly across his nipples, feeling them tighten. The cool air felt wonderful against his heated body, easing the urgency.

She lingered over his back, enjoying the feel of long, lean muscles under her hands. She pulled softly, bringing him down to lie flush against her. One long leg lifted to hook around his hip, pulling him closer. He let his hands trail down her sides and shaped the enticing curve of her behind before tugging on the drawstring loose on her linen drawers and sliding them down her legs. He lifted up slightly to look her over, clad only in her bodice. His fingers went to the knot that held the bodice laces taut but it stubbornly refused to unknot. With an easy chuckle, he gave up on the laces and stroked one breast through the material, toying lazily with her nipple. Aenor lay back and enjoyed the attention, one arm wrapped around his shoulders, her hand stoking the nape of his neck.

The Dragonrider's Quest

Marius bent to tongue a stiff nipple through the fabric of her bodice. The wet fabric turned transparent, showing pink underneath. He blew gently on the wet spot, causing her to gasp as she felt the delightful chill shiver all the way down to her toes. His free hand crept down her front and under her bodice, trying to make it up to her breasts. Alas, the sole purpose of the bodice was support and the tight fabric defied his intentions. Aenor giggled in a very unwarrior-like way as Marius paused and considered the offending garment.

Undaunted, Marius merely changed direction and let his fingers trail further down, heading for her moist center. She parted her thighs invitingly, letting his fingers slip between and dip into the moist flesh there. She was already moist. As he stroked her clitoris with light, delicate strokes, the slippery fluid between his fingertips brought with it provocative images of long, smooth strokes, delicious easy sliding, wetness and heat wrapped around his straining penis.

Aenor's thoughts ran along the same line. She pushed him back and straddled him, fitting his hard cock against her clitoris. She leant forward slightly as she began to rub herself against him. Her fluids spread all over his cock as she maintained a light, teasing stroke. His hands found her breasts through her bodice, flicking and stroking her taut nipples through the textured cloth. The extra simulation got her attention. Her rhythm quickened by a heartbeat as the hands moving on her breasts in tandem with the friction on her clitoris started her reaching for a climax. Marius drank in the pleasure on her face, her eyes closing in absolute focus, keeping her rhythm steady until she groaned her climax softly.

Twenty miles away, in her private cave, Lya jerked awake. Disoriented, she shook her head to clear her mind. When another wave of pleasure came in from her bondmate, her focus immediately shifted to Aenor. Oh. Stifling her thoughts so that Aenor wouldn't be distracted from the business at hand, Lya stealthily hunkered down to experience human mating second-hand.

The sensations coming through the bond felt strangely familiar to Lya. It called to mind the exhilaration of her first flight, and specifically the moment when she leapt off one of the cliffs bordering the Silver Claw warren. There was an unmistakable sense of freedom and joy as the warm thermals from the base of the cliff flowed upwards, filling the leathery membrane of her wings, bearing her up towards the sky. Her bondmate was feeling a similar surge of pleasure, letting go of all fear and just flying fierce and free. As Aenor built towards another climax, it felt to Lya like she was racing towards the sun, heart pumping steadily, flight muscles straining to reach new heights. And yet when the finale came, it was a completely new experience for the dragon.

As Aenor lay draped over Marius, both breathing hard, an unexpected thought came in from Lya. *That was really interesting. Can you do it again?*

Aenor stifled a giggle, flushing red from a combination of embarrassment and lust. *Why yes, Lya... I most certainly can.*

Epilogue

The College of the Healing Arts, North Huria

Six years later

Marius was showing a group of first years the formula for a basic headache remedy, when the sound of several boots thundered past his classroom. His students started fidgeting and twenty earnest faces swung towards him. Marius smiled and jerked his head towards the door. One and all charged out the door. A minute later, with his heart suddenly pounding a lot faster, Marius plastered a benign smile on his face and glided out the door on the heels of his students.

A cluster of apprentices were down the hill, leaning over the fences, gawping at the dragonrider and her dragon. A couple of the braver ones were helping Aenor unload the dragonsaddle while Lya arched her neck and posed like a dignified, blue statue. Lya absolutely adored the attention lavished on her in Huria, although she would have died rather than admit it. Dragons were rare enough here that she was the real attraction, not her rider.

Relieved of all her baggage, Aenor set about unbuckling Lya's harness. By the time, Marius reached the group, Aenor and her assistants had dragged it off Lya's body and spread it out on the grass in a pile of leather and silver. Lya always wore her best harness in Huria. Putting the best talon forward, no doubt.

"Welcome back, instructor" said the Maester as he gripped her forearm in greeting, noting the new captain's insignia on her sleeve. "All is prepared for you."

"It's good to be back, Maester" she replied with exquisite politeness as they started walking back up the hill. Aenor nodded pleasantly to the students, male and female, that she recognized from previous years. Some of the faculty had also emerged from the cloister and they welcomed her with smiles and handshakes. Instructor Merivel arrived twice a year to instruct the journeymen healers on the art of weaponless self-defense. She did so for the unheard-of, low price of a daily cow (for the dragon) and several hours' consultation with the Maester. No doubt, they spent hours discussing their past adventures and if anyone noticed that the instructor's bed was never slept in, they turned a collective blind eye towards that.

After all the formalities were observed, the two of them retired to the Maester's study on the top floor where the pretense dropped soon as the door closed. Her pack fell to the floor as they grabbed each other and fused into a hot, drugging kiss.

Several hours later, a sated Aenor lay on her stomach in Marius's heavy curtained bed. Marius lay on his side beside her, propped up on one elbow, lazily drawing patterns on her lower back with a long finger. She looked up at him. He oozed contentment like a well-fed cat.

"Marius, I'm due for my onset in three months."

"Mmmm hmmm." His smile widened ever so slightly as he waited for her to ask him to be her partner.

"I want to have a baby."

Daphne Ignatius

About the Author

Daphne Ignatius was born and raised in Malaysia. She attended the University of Kansas where she earned a Bachelor's in Computer Engineering and a Masters in Business Administration. The daughter of two high-school teachers, she was instilled with a love of the written word at an early age, and put down her first short story in unreadable long hand at the age of eight. Her earliest remembered ambition was to become an author and that desire resurfaced during an existential crisis, resulting in *The Dragonrider's Quest*.

Daphne currently lives in Atlanta, Georgia with her beloved spouse where she works as an Information Technology professional during her daylight hours. Her existential crisis continues profitably with her second novel, tentatively titled *My Life as Athena*.